After Elise fell asleep, Rose crept to the garden. Ombrine had ordered her to stay out of it—especially at night—and promised severe punishment if she disobeyed.

But it was in this garden she had last seen her mother, and had heard the joyous news that her father was coming home.

"*You are loved,*" the roses whispered.

"I *was* loved," she said brokenly. "But now they're gone." She began to cry again.

Moonlight gleamed around Rose like her mother's sheltering arms, and after a time, she fell into a deep, heavy sleep.

And in that sleep, a glowing hand cupped a shimmering white mouth pressed against her ear.

A voice whispered, "*Alas, daughter of she who made the wish, you still must walk through the shadows until you see the light. Once you learn the lesson, two broken hearts shall mend.*"

Rose slumbered and didn't hear the voice.

But her heart heard it.

Once Upon a Time

THE ROSE BRIDE

A Retelling of "The White Bride and the Black Bride"

By Nancy Holder

SIMON PULSE
New York   London   Toronto   Sydney

This book is a work of fiction. Any references to historical events, real people,
or real locales are used fictitiously. Other names, characters, places, and incidents
are the product of the author's imagination, and any resemblance to actual
events or locales or persons, living or dead, is entirely coincidental.

〰

SIMON PULSE

An imprint of Simon & Schuster Children's Publishing Division
1230 Avenue of the Americas, New York, NY 10020
Copyright © 2007 by Nancy Holder
All rights reserved, including the right of
reproduction in whole or in part in any form.
SIMON PULSE and colophon are registered trademarks
of Simon & Schuster, Inc.
The text of this book was set in Adobe Jenson.
Manufactured in the United States of America
First Simon Pulse edition June 2007
2 4 6 8 10 9 7 5 3 1
Library of Congress Control Number 2007923285
ISBN-13: 978-1-4169-3535-3
ISBN-10: 1-4169-3535-5

To *"Chipmunk" Belle, child of light,*
and her fairy rings:

Club Weirdo:

Haley "Elvis" Schricker, Jesse "Otter" Greenfield, Emily
"Bob Thing" Hogan, Steffi "Staff" Sontgerath, and
Julia "Jules" and Mandy "Mandy-Candy" Escobedo

The Ones Who Were There Before the Beginning:

Grace Beck, Sarah Wilcox, Melody and Mallory
Muehlbauer, and Alexandra and Anna Rose Morel

And with gratitude, love, and deep respect to:

Melanie Tem,
CLG,
and my mother, Marion Elise Smith

Love is much like a wild rose, beautiful and calm,
but willing to draw blood in its own defense.
                              —Mark Overby

Love looks not with the eyes, but with the mind;
And therefore is winged Cupid painted blind.
                              —William Shakespeare

PROLOGUE
Once Upon a Time . . .

In the Land Beyond . . .
Crown Prince Jean-Marc, son of His Royal Majesty
Henri III, Heir to the Throne of the Land Beyond,
Beloved of Zeus, caught his breath as Lucienne,
Princess of the Silver Hills, walked with her ladies and
her priestesses into the airy, domed temple of his god.
Sunshine poured in from the cloudless sky, tinting her
magnificent silver gown with golden light. Over her
braided silvery-blonde hair, she wore a tiara of glittering diamonds and enameled crescent moons, signifying
her devotion to the goddess Artemis.

Her starry midnight-blue eyes gleamed as she
caught sight of Jean-Marc waiting for her at the altar.
He was dressed in ermine robes lined with gold, a
black-and-gold doublet and black hose, and a heavy
gold crown. Jean-Marc's black hair curled around his
ears, revealing the sharp planes and angles of his face,
softened by his smile. His brows were dark, and his
deep-set eyes darker, and filled with rapture as he
gazed at Lucienne, his bride of four months.

The prince had been a solitary youth, left to his
own devices by a father who married a succession of
wives. Each queen had died—Jean-Marc's mother,

1

Marie, had been King Henri's second wife—and the temple of Zeus had consecrated seven royal step-mothers since Jean-Marc's birth. To think that at last the lonely prince had found a boon companion to share his life! Who would have dreamed that the prince and princess, joined together for political reasons, would fall so madly in love? It was enchanting. Miraculous. Surely a gift from the gods.

So it must be that Zeus, presiding in the form of a great marble statue, bearded and broad-chested, looked down on them with favor. Aglow with sunshine and torchlight, was he not smiling?

The chief priest of Zeus stretched forth his arms in greeting. His two assistants flanked him. All three wore white togas bordered with gold, and crowns of laurel pushed low over their foreheads. The head priest was the oldest. On his right stood his associate, a priest in the fullness of his manhood; on the left, a boy acolyte, to signify the youngest age of man.

King Henri, Jean-Marc's father, was not there. The recent widower had been called away on matters of State, but he had toasted his son and daughter-in-law the night before, wishing them both the answer to all their prayers as the three tossed their golden goblets into the flames.

They were about to hear if this month, that prayer would be answered.

The altar was covered with roses of scarlet and creamy ivory—red for the House of the Land Beyond, white for the Silver Hills. Also, vapors of burning incense and towers of gleaming gold coins, payment for the gift of prophecy bestowed upon the three holy men. There were hundreds of coins, all graced with the likeness of Henri, and they would be given to the poor in the name of the king. The Land Beyond was the center of a vast realm and the treasury bulged with taxes and tribute.

Lucienne's three priestesses, dressed in white robes caught at the shoulders with silver stars, wore diadems of the moon in her phases over long white gossamer veils that covered their braids. They carried diamond-studded silver arrows, symbols of their patroness, Artemis, Goddess of the Hunt and of the Moon. The priestess who led the procession was a crone, revered as a wisewoman and midwife. The priestess of childbearing age walked on Lucienne's right. The third priestess, a newly consecrated maiden, held Lucienne's left hand—the one nearer the princess's heart—to give weight to Lucienne's wish to bear the crown prince's son.

As the priestesses reached the altar of their priestly counterparts, they regally inclined their heads and no more, for they were equals. But Lucienne made a full curtsy to the men of Zeus, which included her husband. Moving swiftly, Jean-Marc took his place beside her, and gallantly helped her to her feet.

Jean-Marc laced his fingers through Lucienne's. She squeezed his hand. He couldn't take his eyes off her. Her dark blue eyes widened, framed by her unusual silver-and-gold tresses, and the prince felt as though he were staring into the eyes of Artemis herself. He knew Lucienne had prayed to the Lady the night before and that the tender wishes of her women held great sway with the goddess.

"I have cast the runes," the chief priest of Zeus announced as he lowered his gnarled hands to the altar. The other two priests lifted festoons of roses to reveal a round, beaten-gold tray, and on it, a simple scattering of ancient bone rectangles.

Jean-Marc and Lucienne held their breaths as both stared at the runes. They couldn't read them. No man could, save the one who threw them.

Lucienne's mouth worked silently, praying to Artemis. Their hearts and bodies were new to each other, and yet both hoped, both dared . . .

"I have cast the runes," the priest said again, his voice booming. His words echoed off the white stone columns, and he broke into a smile. "You will have a son in the spring and he will mend two broken hearts."

Lucienne caught her breath and threw her arms around her husband. Aware of the young life inside her, Jean-Marc was afraid to hold her. But as she ecstatically melted against him, he grinned and caught her up, whirling her in a circle beneath the temple dome. She threw back her head and laughed, her golden hair flying behind her head like a cape.

"A son!" cried the priests, as the youngest one raced to the statue of Zeus and hefted the ceremonial torch from the wall. He lit the enormous pile of papery-dry laurel leaves and oak branches in an alabaster bowl at the foot of the god. Smoke billowed and streamed toward the hole in the ceiling.

The priestesses took up the cry, raising their arrows above their heads. "A son!"

Outside the temple, gongs clanged. Bells chimed. Cheers rose up. The kingdom began rejoicing. Riders bolted from the royal stables to carry the news far and wide. The gods were kind. The succession was assured.

"Let's go and receive the blessing of the people," Jean-Marc said, setting her down as if she were made of crystal and tenderly enfolding her hand with both of his. Jean-Marc could scarcely believe his good fortune. A son. His heir.

"First, I must thank the goddess," she reminded him.

"I'll thank her too," Jean-Marc said impetuously.

But as they turned to go, the priest of Zeus cleared his throat and said, "Your Majesties, I ask your pardon, but it occurs to one that the prince might thank Father Zeus first, as *he* is your family's patron."

A shadow crossed Jean-Marc's face, as if the massive statue of his god had shifted on its dais. Jean-Marc gazed up at the statue, and it stared impassively down at him. Chilled, the prince sank at once to his knees.

"*M'excusez*," he murmured. "Of course. I owe my

loyalty and gratitude to the Lord of the Gods." He lowered his head. "Forgive a thoughtless disciple."

"He accepts your apology. He is pleased with you," the priest told Jean-Marc. His features softened. "After all, he's giving you a son."

Jean-Marc smiled at the older man, but his princess looked troubled. She remained silent until the two had left the temple, but as their delighted guards grouped around them, she said softly, "Your god isn't jealous, is he? He won't punish you for forgetting to thank him?"

"Of course he won't punish me," Jean-Marc scoffed. "I'm the son of the Land Beyond. Zeus favors my house."

He put his arm around her shoulders. He could hardly believe it. He had been alone most of his life, but he had a family now.

"The priest said our child would mend two broken hearts," she persisted. "Whose hearts could those be, but ours? Broken because we angered the god?"

"Perhaps they're my heart and my mother's," Jean-Marc replied. "I am told she wept when I was born, because she knew she was going to die." And so she had, three days later.

He spoke without self-pity, but his gentle princess, soon to be a mother herself, slipped her hand into his and said, "I won't leave you. Ever."

"*Merci, ma belle*," he replied, and he suddenly felt a whisper of pain deep in his heart. Confused, he fell silent. This was one of the happiest moments of his life; there was no cause for heartache. He pushed a smile onto his face. He didn't want to dampen Lucienne's joy. It was the dream of queens and princesses everywhere to give birth to an heir, and Lucienne's dream would soon come true.

And she, and he, and their child, would live happily ever after.

Would they not?

ONE

Once upon a time, in the Forested Land, a merchant named Laurent Marchand lived with his second wife, Celestine, and their little daughter, Rose. Laurent toiled endlessly to acquire vast wealth, and Fortune smiled on him. His family lived like nobility in a sprawling slate-roofed *château* that towered above fertile orchards and wild woods teeming with game. They dressed in fine silks and satins and dined on dishes of gold bound with silver. Their servants were happy and counted themselves lucky indeed to work for such a prosperous man.

But as with all forested lands, shadows cast their darkness over the manor on the hill. That was to be expected. Most living things begin in the absence of light: The vine is rooted in the earth; the fawn takes form in the womb of the doe. So it is with secret wounds and heartaches. They can father the greatest happiness—if a brave, shining soul will bear them from the darkness and lift them to the light.

So it is also with the deepest of all joys: a love so true and everlasting that it can heal such wounds. For true love is true magic, as those who have found it can attest.

Laurent's dark, secret wound was named Reginer Marchand. Reginer was Laurent's son by his first wife, who had died giving birth to him. Laurent pinned all his hopes on his heir, waiting for the day when his son would be old enough to help him expand his vast domain. He believed that with Reginer by his side, he would amass a fortune larger than any he could create alone.

But Reginer wanted to be a painter, not a merchant. He spent days, nights, weeks at his easel, reveling in his artistic vision. Thanks to Laurent's efforts, the family would never run out of money, so why sacrifice his dream on the altar of commerce?

Laurent was infuriated by his son's "disloyalty." Painting was a fine pastime, but there was an estate to manage and trading to do. Anger grew on both sides, and one stormy January night, Laurent and Reginer quarreled violently. Reginer packed a bag and stomped out of the grand house. Biting sleet pierced his ermine cloak, and the winter wind wailed like mourners at a funeral.

"Go! Go and be damned!" Laurent yelled, shaking his fist at his son's retreating back. "Though you starve, though your children beg in the streets, never ask a thing of me! Think of me as your father no longer and never dare to put your hand on my door!"

Heartsick and humiliated, Reginer obeyed his

father's command to the letter. Years passed, and he did not return.

When Laurent married his second wife, Celestine, and brought her to the estate, she was sorry to learn of the rift between her new husband and his firstborn. Despite her gentle entreaties, Laurent still refused to forgive Reginer. And as Celestine loved her husband and owed him everything, she promised that she would follow his edict and bar the door to her stepson. But Reginer never came. So the shadow of the wound became invisible, although it was still very real.

The other shadow that fell across the lives of the Marchands was easier to see, although it too, had to do with the aching of the human heart. It was Laurent's near-continuous absence from the beautiful *château* and his family.

"I chase gold as others chase the hare," he boasted to his delicate, fair-haired wife, "and I do so for you and our daughter. My love is such that you will never go wanting."

He didn't understand that Celestine and Rose were sorely wanting indeed: When he was gone, which was more often than not, they missed him terribly. His time and attention were more valuable to them by far than their jewels and dresses. Of a moonlit evening, Celestine would walk along the stony terraces of the *château*, gazing past the topiary garden, the hedge maze, and the chestnut groves to the narrow, winding mountain passes, searching for her husband's retinue. She understood that Laurent loved them, but there were times she felt more widow than wife.

Aside from her beloved child, Celestine's boon companion was Elise Lune, who had served as Celestine's nurse at the family seat on the Emerald Plains. When Celestine married Laurent, the young bride begged Elise to come with her to the Forested Land.

"I shall know no one there," Celestine reminded her. "And one hopes that one will have children, and such tiny blossoms will need tending. . . ."

Elise had no other family and loved Celestine like her own child. So she left the comfort of the Emerald Plains to journey with her young mistress to the Forested Land. She was the first to know that Celestine would have a child and she helped in the delivery of Rose. Many a night she walked the floors of the Marchand mansion, singing lullabies and bouncing the teething child. She was with Celestine when Rose took her first step. And it was she who slipped Celestine's gold coins bearing the likeness of King Henri beneath Rose's pillow whenever the dear girl lost a tooth. She was so beloved that she became *Tante* Elise—Aunt Elise—and the fact that she was a servant slipped from everyone's minds.

When little Rose turned seven, Celestine decided to create a rose garden for her daughter's pleasure. Once the dozens of bushes were planted, Celestine tended them with nearly as much love and devotion as she showered on *la belle* Rose. The roses responded and the garden became an astonishing bower of unearthly beauty, a lush, velvet canopy of crimson hanging over a blanket of scarlet, opulent with heady perfume. Celestine placed two stone statues of young does at the entrance to the grotto and erected a life-size marble statue of the goddess Artemis in the center. Strong, serene Artemis was the Goddess of the Hunt and of the Moon, and Celestine was devoted to her. Artemis watched over women everywhere and offered them protection when and where she could.

Seeking such protection for Rose, Celestine surrounded Artemis with white roses, symbols of her child's innocence and purity. She added a trickling fountain and silvery stream, inviting the wild deer that roamed the manor grounds to drink and rest. And on each lonely night of her vigil for Laurent, she would kneel at the feet of her patroness and pray for his safe return.

The path to the statue grew worn as the years passed. The white rosebushes—indeed, all the rosebushes—flourished into a magical land of their own. Laurent came and went, as was his custom. Mother and daughter were cherished, but usually from afar. Rose became a beautiful girl, an unusual girl, with silvery-gold hair that shimmered like the coin her father pursued, and starry eyes of midnight blue.

On the evening before Rose's thirteenth birthday, the crescent moon shone against the winter sky like Artemis's gleaming bow. The air quivered with anticipation. Laurent had sent dozens of gifts—a music box, a harp, and a tender portrait of a young girl with a white cat—but the most exquisite gift of all was a formal gown of deep rose-colored satin and gold tissue, embroidered with silver stars. Celestine had never seen such a magnificent dress in her entire life, and as she fingered the layers and layers of fabric, she couldn't wait to see Laurent's face when he saw his daughter wearing it. Such attention to detail, such care, assured Celestine that the giver of the gift—Laurent—knew that this dress was meant for someone's Best Beloved—that he loved their child with all his heart.

But she felt a soft pity for him, as well. Celestine knew that as wonderful as the dress and all the other presents might be, the only thing Rose wanted for her birthday was her father. And this, Celestine suspected, he did not know. He counted his worth in the things he could give them, and not in himself, their beloved husband and father. He would probably be most amazed to know that Rose had been counting the days until her birthday not so she could have her gifts, but in the hopes that he would put his arms around her and hold her close.

Indeed, her sweet daughter had embroidered a fine purple cloak for him, to thank him for the gift of life. Rose had stitched thirteen roses on the border, leaving room for more years to come. It lay among the gifts he had sent to her and she couldn't wait to give it to him.

Sunset after sunset Rose stood on the watchtower, waiting for him. He didn't come. As the evening became night and then midnight on the eve of her birthday, there was no still sign of him.

Celestine was determined not to let the terrible disappointment mar the dawn. "I call on you, my patroness," she murmured as she scattered dried white rose petals before the marble statue. It was the beginning of winter, and the hands of all the bushes, including the white ones, had been trimmed back. Their fingertips were painted with frost. "Goddess," she prayed, "give Rose a gift as she enters the sisterhood of women. Send Laurent home for her birthday."

The crescent moon rippled, and a spray of shooting stars cascaded like a falling arrow over the craggy mountaintops.

A night breeze sighed against Celestine's ear as if to say, "*I cannot force the actions of another.*"

"Alas," Celestine murmured as the last of the petals drifted from her fingertips. "Then, at least, please let her know her father loves her."

"*I cannot guarantee the heart of another,*" the breeze replied.

"*My* heart is guaranteed," she pledged. "Let her know *my* heart. Let her know that she is loved with a love that is true and will never fade as the rose petal fades. If she knows that, it will be all that she needs in this life."

"*That is your request? Is that the gift she will have for her birthday?*" asked the breeze.

"*Oui*," Celestine replied.

"*You desire this for your daughter beyond riches?*" asked the breeze. "*Is it better to know that you are loved or to live in plenty?*"

"It's better to know that you are loved," Celestine answered. Who knew the answer to that question better than she? "A woman who is loved is the richest woman on earth."

As she spoke, a dappled fawn cautiously entered the rose grotto, gazed at her with its large brown eyes, and hesitantly approached the stream. Celestine stood motionless, so as not to frighten the sweet little creature.

The fawn lowered its head and lapped at the water.

"*And what of safety? Is it better to know that you are loved or to know that you are safe?*" the breeze challenged her.

"It's better to know that you are loved," Celestine whispered, watching the deer. "There's no greater harbor than that."

"*What if death takes the one who loves you? Then love is gone and you have nothing.*"

"True love never dies," she insisted. "It lives beyond the grave, in the heart of the beloved."

"*That is what you wish your daughter to know?*"

"*Oui*," she said again. "Then she'll be rich and safe for all her days."

The moonlight shifted above her, casting her in a shower of light. The luxurious scent of roses wafted around her, although there were no blossoms on the branches. She gazed up at the moon and then back where the fawn had been drinking.

The creature had turned snow-white and it was glowing like the moon itself. As it lifted its head and gazed at her, she saw that its eyes were dark blue, like Rose's.

"*You have the wisdom of Athena and the heart of Demeter,*" the breeze declared. "*Best Beloved, it shall be as you wish.*"

Something tugged hard at her heart, stealing a beat from it. Her lips parted as she pressed her hand against her chest.

Where the shimmering fawn had stood, a luminous being appeared, shining from crown to heel as if it too, were made of moonbeams. A silver bow was slung over its left shoulder, along with a quiver of arrows made of light. Perhaps it was Eros, God of Love.

Celestine shielded her eyes; the figure was so bright that she could hardly look at it. She felt another tug on her heart and she lost another beat.

"*Fear not. It is done,*" said the luminous figure. "*Go and fetch your child. Bring her here. Leave her nurse asleep. Quickly, before the dawn, or your wish will not come true.*"

The being raised its right arm and pointed toward the topmost turret of the *château*, where Rose slept. Beyond the circular roof, the hem of the sky was growing light.

Celestine dropped a curtsy. Then she turned and skirted the silvery stream, racing past the double statues of deer at the grotto's entrance. At last she dashed into the *château*, startling the night watch. She raced to her daughter's pink-and-white chamber and opened the door.

Her breath caught at the sight of her child, asleep in her canopy bed of creamy satin hangings embroidered with roses. The first hint of morning filtered through the stained glass windows, brushing Rose's petal-soft skin with feathery kisses.

"*Bonjour*, Rose," Celestine murmured, rousing her daughter ever so gently. "It is your birthday, my love. The happiest day of my life. Come to the garden and receive your special gift."

"*Maman?*" Rose said drowsily as she opened her deep blue eyes. They widened; hope danced in them. "Is Papa here?"

"Not quite yet." She held her close.

Rose's lower lip trembled and she looked away to hide a tear.

"The day is young," Celestine said.

"*Oui, Maman*," Rose replied, but the tear sparkled like a diamond.

"Come with me." Celestine reached for Rose's ermine cloak and fleece-lined leather slippers. "There is magic in the air." She helped Rose out of bed and wrapped her in the warm cloak and slippers.

"Magic? What magic?" Rose asked.

"Birthday magic," her mother answered, leading her out of her room. "Let's wake up Tante Elise." She rapped softly on the nurse's door. The snoring continued. Celestine knew they must hurry and she wished she'd thought to awaken Elise first. She decided to let her sleep, mindful of the being's command to bring Rose to the garden before the dawn.

"We'll come back for her in a little while," Celestine said.

Like naughty children, they tiptoed through the sleeping household, down the circular staircase, moving so fast that Celestine felt dizzy and almost missed a step.

Snow sprinkled their bare heads as they ran breathlessly out the door, past the topiary figures dusted with snowflakes: a dragon, a gryphon, a lion. A lark trilled. A wind whipped up, sweeping the snow from their path as they tripped through the hedge maze. They turned left and left again, leaving the grandeur of the *château* behind, to enter the wintry simplicity of the bare rose garden.

They froze in their tracks.

"What is this?" Celestine whispered.

All the bushes had burst into full bloom. The grotto was a trove of color. Fiery curtains of orange and crimson petals pooled on top of the snowbanks. Pinks dotted the overhanging clusters of billowy yellow. Ivory blossoms piqued the snow like rosettes on a wedding gown.

"*Maman*, it's so beautiful!" Rose whirled in a circle, her ermine cloak making a disc of white around her. Damascene moonlight and sunshine glowed against her eager face. "What a gift! *Merci, Maman!*"

Celestine gazed this way and that, searching for the luminous being. But neither it nor the shimmering fawn was anywhere to be seen.

How can this be? Celestine silently asked the statue.

As if in answer, tears welled in the statue's eyes. Tears? On a joyful occasion such as this? Frightened, Celestine felt her heart tug again, much harder this time. She lost three beats at once.

The tears spilled from the marble eyes onto a spray of white roses, and they immediately turned a subtle shade of blue.

"*Maman,* look!" Rose cried. Unaware of her mother's confusion and of the weeping statue, she picked one of the blue roses and held it out to Celestine. But as Celestine reached for it, her chest seized again and her hand jerked. She pricked her finger on the blue rose's thorn, and three droplets of blood fell onto the azure petals.

A rich, deep purple spread through the petals like blood through veins.

"You are wounded!" Rose cried as she dropped the flower. It fell onto the bush. The color seeped from that blossom to the next, and to the next, until all the roses on the bush were the same vibrant shade.

And in that moment, Celestine knew that she was dying. Her wish had set her death in motion, and her request was to be her last.

"Rose," Celestine said urgently as she sank against the soft pillows of snow, "listen to me."

"What is happening? What's wrong?" Rose demanded, dropping to her knees beside her. "I'll go for help!"

"No. Stay. Listen," Celestine ordered her. Her words came with difficulty as she gasped for breath. "The purple roses. They're your birthday gift. They're my promise that you are loved with real, true love. Remember that. Love is real and it is the greatest gift, and it is yours."

"What are you saying?" Rose asked shrilly as Celestine's eyes flickered and the light began to leave them. She threw back her head and cried to the last traces of the night, "Help! Tante Elise! *Au secours!*"

"*Attends.* Listen," her mother whispered. She gripped Rose hard, with the desperation of one who is putting to sea on the barge of the dead, yet has unfinished business in the land of the living. "No matter your griefs or your sorrows, your trials or your fate, always remember: *Ma belle, ma petite,* you are loved." She began to weep as Rose's image grew fainter and more distant. "Never forget. You are loved."

"*Maman!*" Rose screamed, understanding at last that her mother was dying. "Don't leave me!"

"You will always have my love," Celestine gasped. "Always."

Rose burst into tears, leaning over her mother, embracing her, kissing her, willing her to stay in the mortal world. She rocked her and begged her and wept for what seemed like years.

The deer statues at the entrance to the garden lowered their heads. The goddess sighed. As the blazing chariot of Apollo galloped on the horizon, Celestine Marchand breathed her last.

The roses in the bower immediately withered and died—all save the purple rosebush. Golden sunshine gilded the magic petals, and they whispered to the distraught girl:

"*You are loved.*

"*You are loved.*

"*You are loved.*"

Two

By midday, Monsieur Valmont, the elegant old majordomo, sent riders to bear the news of Madame's death to Laurent and bid him to speed home. Elise laid out the still-lovely Celestine, dressing her in her white wedding gown, combing and arranging her hair. Weeping, she sprinkled dried rose petals over the intricate lace of her lady's bridal veil. Between Celestine's dead hands, Elise placed a miniature portrait of Laurent and a plaited knot of Rose's hair.

She wrapped Rose's splendid pink dress in tissue and muslin and put it away.

Wrapped in ebony mourning with Elise at her side, Rose drooped beside her mother's bier in the *château*'s temple to Hermes. Laurent was a disciple of the god.

Elise held Rose's hand, but Rose was too numb to feel it.

A week dragged by. Two. Three.

Laurent didn't come. The messengers reported that he was nowhere to be found. Celestine retained her beauty, as if she were only sleeping.

Night and day Rose watched Celestine's unmoving chest, willing her to breathe. But she never did. Her heart did not beat and her skin was as cold as the icy burial vault.

The new moon rose, signaling the death of the first month of winter. More messengers rode out. They came back empty-handed. Elise begged Rose to come away, to take more than a sip of soup, to rest.

"I am here. I will care for you," Elise promised, but Rose could not hear the words. She would not budge.

The *château's* priest explained to Rose that her mother had a journey to make and Rose must let her go. As things stood, her mother's spirit could not move forward and it could not return.

"But I love her," Rose whispered.

The priest was a wise man and a gentle teacher. He said, "It's not your love that holds her hostage. It's your need. True love wants, but it doesn't need. True love thinks of the beloved first."

So she agreed to bury her mother.

Banshee winds howled as Celestine's marble sarcophagus was sanctified and sealed in the burial vault of Château Marchand. Draped over the lid, Rose wept until her ribs ached. She had no idea how she would endure the pain that seized her heart as surely as the God of Death had seized her mother's.

"It's over now, my darling," Elise murmured to her. Her cheeks were wet. Her black wimple framed her round face, taut with grief. "She is at peace. And we must find joy in that."

But it was not over. The servants muttered among themselves about a father who wouldn't come home to comfort his own daughter. About a man who was seen in a tavern, drinking mead, with a woman on his lap.

"There's an explanation for why he hasn't come," Elise promised. "A good one. Although I'm sure he's well," she added hastily. "And safe."

But he didn't send word and he didn't return.

Night after night, beneath the harsh winter snows, Rose crept to the garden and fell to her knees before the only flowers that blossomed—the purple roses. In gauzy moonlight and bitter snowstorm, they whispered, *"You are loved, you are loved."* But Rose's broken heart could scarcely hear the words.

Night after night Elise searched for Rose and found her. She held her in her arms and crooned lullabies, as she had when she was a babe. But her comfort was as insubstantial as a phantom, and Rose could not be consoled.

Two more moons waxed and waned and the seasons changed. It was springtime and all the roses in Celestine's garden flowered into rainbows of red, pink, and white. The single purple rosebush eclipsed all the other roses in its glory. Rose breathed in the scent as the velvety petals caressed her cheeks. She heard the petals murmur, *"You are loved, you are loved."*

But she believed them not at all.

Five months passed and Laurent still did not come. On the last night of summer as the sun fell, Rose sat at the feet of Artemis. She hunched over the cloak she had embroidered for her father for her birthday five months before. She was almost thirteen and a half, so there was time for a fourteenth rose, but she imagined that when she worked on it, she was drawing him to her. Her fingers were dotted with pricks from her needle, but the pain was not as great as that in her heart.

She worked on it as often as she could in the shelter of the grotto. There she couldn't hear the cook and the upstairs maid gossiping about the sad state of affairs on the estate. She couldn't see Monsieur Valmont using her mother's ring of keys to unlock the silver closet. He was taking her precious dishes from the pantry one at a time and only as needed, to sell so that he could pay the servants. Celestine had always managed the estate when her father was gone, and now that she was gone, no one knew what to do. Monsieur Valmont's position had been like that of a valet, seeing to the comfort of *monsieur, madame,* and *mademoiselle.* He had no head for business.

In the garden, the purple roses whispered, *"You are loved."*

Smoothing her black velvet waistcoat and black silk skirts, Rose leaned forward into the center of the bush. She clutched the folds of the cloak as the velvety purple petals brushed her cheeks like butterfly kisses. She closed her eyes and imagined her mother kissing her, and tears streamed down her face.

"You are loved. You are loved," the roses murmured.

"It doesn't matter," she murmured to them. "I am afraid."

"You are loved."

"We're losing our home. Will love bring it back?"

She thought she heard the night breeze whisper something about wishes and journeys. She tipped her head and looked up at the statue of Artemis, strong and silent, who seemed to gaze urgently at her as if to say, *Learn the lesson and we are done.*

"What is it you wish me to learn, madame?" she asked the statue.

The figure made no answer, and the moonlight shifted, draping her features in shadow.

Rose wiped away her tears and again grabbed her needle. She was hard at work when she heard the bells and the shouting and pressed her lips together, too hopeful even to hope.

"Rose? Rose!" Elise called in the distance. "It is your father!"

With a gasp, Rose jumped up, gathering the cloak against her chest with shaking hands. Something caught at her hem. It was a purple rose, thorns embedded in the velvet like the fingers of a little child yanking on her skirt.

"You are loved," the rose whispered to her.

She bent down and freed her skirt. Her hair rippling behind her, she ran past the silver stream, through wave after wave of roses, bounding like a fawn. Then she galloped past the deer statues at the entrance of the grotto, where Elise raced toward her.

"Can it be?" Rose cried.

"*Oui!*" Elise replied.

They fell into each other's arms, embracing, laughing, weeping. In the dark afternoon, the servants swarmed around them as everyone hurried to the *château*. Seeing Rose's joy, they burst into cheers and applause.

She and Elise climbed the stairs to the watchtower. Elise huffed and puffed as the two flew up, up, and up like butterflies, and finally burst out the door. Monsieur Valmont was there. It was he who had been ringing the bell.

"*Voilà!* Look!" he cried, pointing to the craggy mountains in the distance.

"*Où?*" Rose demanded. "Where?"

She leaned over the wall, searching for the parade of horses against the bright orange sunset. Far away, shapes moved against the carpets of mustard plants and lavender. Horses and riders, navigating the treacherous mountain road.

"I see them!" she cried, embracing first Elise and then Monsieur Valmont. The faithful man was crying with joy, tears streaming down his thin, wrinkled cheeks.

"At last, at last," Monsieur Valmont said. "I have prayed to Hermes for this day."

"And we to Artemis!" Rose said, grabbing Elise's hand and squeezing it. Her old nurse was weeping as well.

Rose rushed back to the parapet and placed her

fingers against her lips to blow her father a kiss, just as the dying sun dipped below the hills. And in that very moment, it was as if the axis of the earth shifted and the scales of Libra lost their balance. Colors bleached to gray and white. The temperature dropped like a stone off a cliff.

She slowly lowered her hand and touched her neck; her pulse fluttered. Despite the cold, her forehead beaded and her cheeks tingled with feverish heat.

"Something is wrong," she murmured, unable to swallow past the tightness in her throat. "Something is wrong with my father."

Elise cocked her head and raised her finger as if she were testing the wind. She reached forward and cupped Rose's cheek.

"*Mais non,*" she said gently. "No. Everything is fine." She cupped Rose's chin and turned it in the direction of the riders. "See? There he is."

But as Rose stared into the gathering darkness, she knew something *was* wrong. She was no stranger to tragedy and she recognized the cold hand of death on the back of her neck.

"All is well," Monsieur Valmont assured her.

"Please," she whispered, "bring him home to me."

There was no answer in the breeze.

Night fell and Rose's father didn't arrive. Elise explained that he had probably made camp. The mountain pass was narrow and difficult. It showed prudence to wait for the morning light.

"He's in danger. We must ride to him," Rose begged. "Please, let's get some of the men and saddle horses—"

"Go to bed, *ma petite*," Elise urged her, bringing her a goblet of wine and a muslin nightdress. "Your father will wake you when he comes."

Then the old lady glided from the room into her own chamber and shut the door. When Elise finally blatted out a snore, Rose leaped out of bed and ran to the chest where her beautiful birthday dress was kept. She caught her breath. She'd forgotten how exquisite it was. The gold sparkled; the deep rose hummed as if with life. The silver embroidery gleamed in the light of her candle.

She tore off her nightdress and lifted up the wondrous gown. Then she pulled it over her head. She wanted to look like a princess for her father. She hoped to soften the blow of the loss of his wife.

As the fragile fabric floated around her shoulders, she reconsidered. The gown was very delicate, feather-light as could be. It was cold tonight and she had hard riding ahead. She didn't want to ruin it.

With regret, she took it off and laid it carefully back on her bed. She would put it on as soon as they returned home together. Making haste, she shimmied into one of her black mourning dresses and draped a heavy traveling cloak over her shoulders. She pulled on black leather riding boots and gloves.

Elise's heavy snores covered the squeak in the floor as Rose tiptoed out of her room. Downstairs, she dodged Monsieur Valmont, who was bellowing commands at the scullery maid. Then she crept into the larder and grabbed a handful of sugar cubes from the silver covered dish.

Then she sneaked out the back door to the stable.

The little mop-haired stable boy was asleep in the hay. Rose walked on the balls of her feet past him to the row of bridles hanging from a row of pegs. She unfastened the harness of Douce, her little mare. The petite gray chuffed softly as Rose approached, stomping the hay-strewn floor in welcome.

"*Hssst, ma belle,*" Rose whispered as she pushed the sugar cubes against Douce's nostrils. Douce sniffed the tantalizing aroma and eagerly gobbled them down. Rose cupped the horse's soft mouth and eased in the bit. Douce took it, and Rose rubbed her forelock in gratitude.

Then she picked up a lantern and quietly led Douce out of the stable beside the geranium-covered wall. She lit the lantern; then, gathering up her skirts, she climbed onto the wall and slung one leg across Douce. She hadn't ridden bareback in years, but she didn't want to risk waking anyone by saddling her mount.

She and Douce quickly found their rhythm as she walked the horse through the silent wheat fields behind the *château*. Douce bobbed her head, as eager as Rose to gallop away. Rose pressed her knees hard against Douce's sides, ordering her to take it slow. She wanted no one to hear the report of Douce's horseshoes clopping against the earth. As it was, her heart beat so loudly she imagined it would awaken the night watchmen. She worried that the bubble of light from the lantern would betray them, but clouds obscured the moonlight and she didn't know the way well enough to ride blind.

An owl hooted, startling her.

Ducking her head, Rose murmured, "Goddess Artemis, keep us safe," and kissed the side of her forefinger to seal the prayer.

Douce shook her withers, and Rose leaned forward to give the horse a comforting pat. She gazed over her shoulder at the large dark shape of the *château*. Here and there, windows glowed with a halo of amber—servants were preparing her father's wing of the house, making sure everything was presentable for his inspection.

Perhaps it might be better to go back. What was she doing, riding out alone in the dark?

"I'm doing what I must," she whispered. It didn't matter if it was the safe thing or the wise thing or even the right thing. It was what she must do. What her heart told her to do.

Raising her chin, she squared her shoulders and rode past the scarecrow.

Où? Où vas-tu? the wind whispered to Rose.

The stars shifted overhead. The owl had taken flight long ago and tiny creatures skittered in the bushes along the familiar path toward the village.

The night pressed down on Rose like a weighty hand. She was fatigued already.

Moments later, she reached a little wooden shrine where people could say prayers for the safe delivery of Princess Lucienne of the Land Beyond. She was carrying the son of Crown Prince Jean-Marc. His father, King Henri, ruled the Forested Land as well as the Land Beyond, but the Forested Land was only a province. The Land Beyond was where he lived.

Rose raised the lantern and inspected the shrine. A thick, tallow candle had been set in front of a foot-tall figurine of a woman. It had blown out. Impulsively Rose opened the door of her own lantern, picked up the tallow candle, and relit its wick with her little flame. Steadying Douce, she leaned over and set it in front of the figure.

"Health and long life to the lady princess and her child," she whispered.

Then she took the fork that led to the mountains. The path was pitch-black, save for the distant star field lining the dome of the sky. Rose guided Douce carefully around sharp curves and switchbacks, holding the lantern up high.

"Papa?" she called. Her voice echoed off the mountainside. There was no answer and she moved ahead.

The mountain to her right dropped away and she licked her lips as the lantern light revealed a sheer drop into a chasm. At the next sharp curve, billows of fog tumbled over the road like the stream of silvery water in the rose garden. It became so heavy she couldn't see her gloved hands gripping the reins.

Uneasily she dismounted, anxiously placing her foot on the firm ground, relieved that she and Douce didn't plunge into empty space.

"It's all right." Her voice quavered. "We're safe." She had no idea if that were true, but she had to keep Douce calm. If her horse panicked, she might leap off the path to her destruction.

Rose stood tense and alert for a long time. Then the lantern candle guttered out, casting Rose and her little gray in utter darkness. Rose bit her lower lip to keep from crying out, and she gave the lantern a tiny shake, hoping that perhaps the wax had flooded the wick and it was still partially lit. But it was clearly out for good. She wished she'd taken the princess's candle instead of relighting it.

"I'm going to call for Papa again, *ma Douce,*" she told the horse as she set the lantern down. With her free hand, she gave the horse a soothing rub so that she wouldn't startle when Rose yelled.

But then she realized that the fog was just as thick for him as it was for her. If he heard her and tried to come for her, he might get hurt, or worse. She felt horribly foolish. She'd set out on this journey to rescue him and now she was the one who needed help. Elise had been right. She should have waited.

She shouldn't have listened to her heart.

Rose had no idea how much time passed, but she began to sway, her gloved hand sliding off Douce's back and her eyes drooping shut, no matter how many times she tried to keep them open. With the reins still in her fist, she felt around until she rested her back against the slimy rock face and slid, weary and done in, onto her bottom.

Wind whistled in her ears, and snowflakes fluttered down. A snowstorm in spring was not unheard of, but the day had been so fair. Snowflakes stuck to her hair and landed on her shoulders. She shivered hard and lowered her head to pray, but instead, she began to drowse.

As her head bobbed, she dreamed that she was standing amid hundreds of purple roses. They were whispering to her, "*You are loved, you are loved.*"

Filled with wonder, she moved slowly in a circle beneath a silvery shaft of moonlight. Her face was raised to the light and she was smiling.

Then a little brown doe stepped from among the opulent curtains and carpets of roses. Its round, elegant head was crowned with purple roses and it carried a single purple blossom by the stem in its mouth. When its dark brown eyes met Rose's, it turned a shimmering white, and its eyes became dark blue, like hers. Then it transformed yet again, into a luminous being of light, armed with a bow and a quiver of arrows.

It held the purple rose in its hand.

It whispered, "*I came from your lady, from Artemis. This journey will be hard. You may falter and you may give up. That is your choice. But if you stop, you stop before journey's end. And it is the journey your mother's wish has set you on. If you will but carry the wound into the light, her dying wish will be granted. You are loved. If you undertake this journey, you will know that. And I promise you, little one, that is worth knowing."*

The being held out the rose.

"Do you accept it?"

"Oui," Rose said, in her dream on the cold mountain pass.

She reached out her hand to take the rose.

THREE

"Fear not. It is done."

Who spoke against Rose's ear?

"Papa?" Rose murmured into the warmth and joy and love. She had found him and her father was cradling her, calling her his own. He loved her. He loved her more than anything. . . .

"Oh, child, child," Elise sobbed, rocking her back and forth.

Rose opened her eyes. She had been dreaming. It was her nurse who was holding her, not her father, and she was in her room, not on the mountain path.

"Papa!" she cried, trying to ease out of Elise's tight embrace. But Elise wouldn't let her go.

Over Elise's shoulder, a long, pale face floated in the darkness like a ghost's. It was a woman's face, with unusually high cheekbones and deep hollows beneath. Slashes of black eyebrows arched over each eye. The lids were heavy and the eyes themselves, fathomless, ebony pools. As the face drew near, it became a woman, dressed in a hooded black travel-ing cloak. In her free hand she held a black scarf embroidered with the initials LM in red.

Laurent Marchand.

"I am Ombrine," the woman said, biting off each syllable in a strangled voice as she twisted the scarf between her hands. Her French was heavily accented. "Ombrine Marchand. Your stepmother."

Rose was astounded. Her heart thundered as she struggled to throw back the bedcovers and get to her feet. Her father, where was her father?

"Papa?" Rose rasped, searching the room with her gaze.

"He is dead," Ombrine said flatly. "Laurent Marchand is dead." Her features hardened; her brows drew across her forehead. "And you killed him."

"No!" Rose cried and leaped out of bed. "Papa! Papa!"

Then the fever hit her, and she crumpled to the floor.

"He was on his way home for your birthday," Ombrine explained to Rose, her heavily lidded eyes downcast as she touched Laurent's handkerchief to her thin, bright-red lips. The lady was seated in a chair beside Rose's bed. Elise had forced Rose back into bed and brought her a cup of wine, wrapping Rose's hand around the stem of the cup with her own and tipping it back against Rose's mouth. But Rose was too ill and shocked to drink. The wine sat on the table beside her bed, untouched.

Desirée, Ombrine's fourteen-year-old daughter, stood beside her mother's chair, her hand on

Ombrine's elegant, straight shoulder. She looked like Ombrine, her black hair pulled back into a braid, revealing a long face of pale skin dominated by a high forehead and enormous, flinty eyes. Like her mother, she wore a black cloak.

Black became them well.

"When Laurent learned of your mother's tragic end," Ombrine continued, "he collapsed on the road. Some huntsmen found him and brought him to me. They thought he was dead, but I revived him. He lay in a stupor for nearly four months."

"Four months is a very long time," Desirée said.

"I devoted myself to his care, day and night, and I nursed him back to health. My own husband ... my *previous* husband ... died more than a year ago, and so it seemed ... perfect. . . ." Her voice caught, and she lowered the handkerchief to her lap.

"There, there, Mother," Desirée murmured as if she were bored. "You have suffered so."

Ombrine glanced sharply at her daughter. Then she turned her attention back to her handkerchief.

"I am not complaining. I *told* him to stay abed. I told him he could send a messenger to let you know what had happened and to say that he would be home as soon as he was well enough to travel. But he wouldn't have it. 'No time for delay,'" she said, mimicking Laurent's deep voice. "He was extremely worried."

Ombrine turned her gaze to Rose. "Worried about you."

You are loved. She could almost hear the purple roses whispering the words to her.

"About me," she whispered.

"*Oui*," Ombrine declared. "He was *very* worried about you. He said you were high-strung and not very . . . resourceful. He was fearful that you'd let the estate go to rack and ruin."

Crushed, Rose slumped against her pillows. The room rocked crazily. Hot tears clouded her vision. Had that truly been his only concern? The estate?

Ombrine shifted in her chair and fingered the nearest creamy rose hanging, narrowing her eyes, seeing something there that Rose did not.

"I see that the deterioration has begun," Ombrine snapped. "Or perhaps it was never quite as grand as he described it." She gave the hanging a flick of her fingers.

"It's not bad," Desirée ventured. Then, at a look from her mother, she cleared her throat. "Although, not quite as grand as my stepfather said."

Ombrine continued, sitting straight on a spine of iron. Her face floated in the dull light, her features blending with the shadows.

"So. Dear Laurent insisted on coming here with all due haste. He was still so weak. . . . When you were found this morning on the mountain pass, sick and in a faint, he thought you were dead. We all did. It was too much for him. His heart gave way." She began to weep. "And now *he's* dead."

"There, there, Mother," Desirée purred.

Rose burst into heavy sobs.

"*Non, non, ma petite*," Elise said, enfolding Rose in her arms. "It was not like that. He came because he loved you so and couldn't wait to see you."

"I killed him!" Rose moaned.

"*Oui*," Ombrine replied. "It is so."

"Madame, *please*," Elise entreated.

"It's better to have it all out at once," Ombrine retorted. "And I will not have impertinence, do you understand?"

Elise pressed Rose hard against her bosom and raised her chin. "Madame, with all due respect." Her voice shook and she held Rose so tightly that Rose couldn't breathe. "I was told her father died in the afternoon. On the road, before the search party found Rose."

"Are you calling me a liar?" Ombrine asked in a cold, dangerous voice.

"She is, Mother," Desirée assured her.

Rose clung to Elise, drowning. A tiny part of her knew that Elise was in trouble and she was afraid for her. If indeed this was her stepmother . . . but how could her father have a new wife? Less than half a year of mourning . . . how could he?

It was all wrong. Everything was wrong. False . . .

"For the love of the gods, give her the wine, if it will help to calm her down. In fact . . ." Ombrine reached into an inner pocket of her cloak and pulled out a small gold vial studded with rubies. She flicked open the hinged lid with her red fingertip. "Give it to me."

Silently Elise handed her the goblet. Ombrine tilted the vial, and a black, viscous liquid seeped out. The first large, thick drop hung from the lip, then plopped into the wine.

Ombrine put in three more drops. Then she snapped the lid shut and put the vial back in her sleeve.

"*Et voilà*," she said.

Elise took it. Studying it, she hesitated and said to Rose, "You're calmer now, eh, *mon enfant*? You don't need this?"

Despite her wild grief, Rose heard the urgency in her nurse's voice. Elise didn't want Rose to drink the wine. She didn't trust Ombrine.

"*Give it to her*," Ombrine bit off. "Or I'll have you whipped for your disobedience."

"I'll take it, madame," Rose said quickly. But as she took the cup, she pretended to hiccup and let go of it. The goblet crashed to the floor, spraying wine in a flume.

"Ah, *non*!" Ombrine cried. Her ebony skirts rustled as she leaped to her feet.

"I am sorry!" Elise said, taking the blame.

"It is as he said. Everyone here is dim-witted and clumsy," Ombrine muttered. "Well, no matter to me. This is an old cloak and I have others. But this . . . *was* one of a kind."

She swept a graceful motion downward to the floor and gathered something up that must have fallen off the bed.

Rose cried out. It was her magnificent birthday

gown. The starry skirt showed a purple wine stain the size of an embroidery hoop. Ombrine folded the delicate fabric in half, then in half again, then again.

"At any rate, you won't be needing it," she said, turning away with the gown crumpled like a rag against her chest.

Desirée trailed after her. "Give it to me," she urged.

"Nonsense," Ombrine told her daughter. "It's ruined."

"We can cut it down," Desirée said, digging her fingers into the dainty tissue. "I've not had such a lovely thing in ever so long, Mother. Before the fire—"

Ombrine's icy stare moved from Desirée's fingers to her face. "Show some decency. We're all in mourning."

Ombrine stopped at the door and waited for Desirée to open it.

With a huff, Desirée stabbed her thumb against the handle and yanked open the door. "He wasn't *my* father."

As soon as the door was shut, Rose begged Elise to help her get out of bed. Her forehead was burning.

"Take me to him. It's a mistake. It's not my father."

Elise sniffled as she laced up the back of Rose's gown. When she was done, she laid a hand on Rose's shoulder.

"I saw him, *ma petite*. It is Laurent. His own physician has signed a death certificate, and—"

"Don't say that," Rose begged. "It's a trick. That horrible woman has arranged all this. My father wouldn't . . . he wouldn't *die*."

Elise cupped Rose's face with her hands and stared hard into her eyes. "*Attends-moi.* Listen to me, my darling. *You did not kill him.* No matter what happens next, it was not your fault."

But Elise's words carried no more weight than a whisper on a breeze.

The funeral was arranged at lightning speed. Monsieur Valmont had taken the liberty of sending riders to invite the masters and mistresses of the nearby estates to the funeral. Ombrine was livid, insisting that she was unprepared to meet her new neighbors in the midst of tragedy.

Laurent's corpse lay on a bier in the family vault, and Rose could not deny that it was he. His skin was waxy and gray. His dear cheeks were sunken. He looked dead, but Celestine had told Rose stories of people who appeared to be dead, only to revive when someone who truly loved them gave them a kiss. So Rose bent over him and kissed his cheek. His skin was ice-cold. Life had left him.

Choked with despair, she ran from the vault and raced to the rose garden. Rose pressed her face into the purple blossoms and inhaled their perfume. They smelled like her mother.

The bitterest tears came, and she clenched her fists against her terror and her despair as the roses whispered to her, "*You are loved. You are loved.*"

"I'm not."

She fell against the ground and wept, her fingers

digging into the soil as if she would climb into the earth and hide in the darkness there forever.

"*You are loved,*" the roses insisted.

Elise found her an hour later. Her skirts furled wide, she ran to Rose's side and lifted her from the mud. She ran her fingers through Rose's silvery-golden hair, plaiting it quickly.

"Your . . . that *woman* wants you at the funeral feast," the nurse said. She wiped Rose's dirty cheeks and hands with her apron. "*Vite, ma belle.* She's very angry."

She led her to the silvery stream, and Rose looked at her reflection. Her starry midnight-blue eyes stared back at her, puffy from weeping. Elise dipped the hem of her apron into the water and washed her face. Rose was beyond caring what she looked like and whether or not her new stepmother was angry with her.

"That's better," Elise said, appraising her young lady. "Now . . ." She looked left and right, then put her finger to her lips. Then she lifted up her black skirts, revealing Rose's birthday gown tied like a petticoat around her waist. It sparkled and glittered as she gathered up the skirts. "We can embroider a beautiful rose over the stain. It will be purple, like your favorite roses."

"Oh," Rose cried softly. "Oh, Elise, *merci.*" She thought then of the cloak she had been stitching for her father, and she had laid it across him in his sarcophagus.

"Not a word," Elise warned her, smoothing down her skirt and pulling her dear young lady into her arms. "Tragedy will turn to triumph. Your dress will be even more lovely than before. And the tide of all this misfortune will turn as well. You'll see."

Elise walked Rose into the great hall, where the feast had been set. There were two dozen guests milling in a hall meant to hold two hundred. Most of the servants were not present, although Rose knew it was the Marchand custom to share the feast with everyone on all the important days. A few moved among the guests, pouring mulled wine into Celestine's golden goblets. The main table, which was yards long, was covered with her mother's most precious white silk tablecloth, and set with what was left of her precious dishes. It was spectacular. Haunches of venison and pork steamed on gold platters; cinnamon, cardamom, and nutmeg thickened the air. There were bowls of potatoes and vegetables and towers of sugared fruits. Rose had no idea how Ombrine had managed to arrange such an elaborate feast on such short notice.

"There she is," Elise murmured.

Ombrine had changed into another gown of black lace and black silk with a plunging neckline. Like an elegant spider, she held court in Celestine's favorite ivory silk-covered chair, a full plate of untouched food at her elbow. She daubed her eyes as a gentleman leaned over her, offering her a goblet of wine. The Widow Marchand wrapped her hand around the man's and gave him a sad smile. His eyes glittered as he leaned closer. Then his gaze dropped toward her ample bosom.

"She's already after another one," Elise said under her breath. She turned to Rose and cupped her cheek. "Well, dear one, we all do what we think we must. Try to find your way in this. I'll stay close by."

Rose took a breath and looked at Ombrine, who was clearly very busy. Then she looked for Ombrine's daughter.

Framed by the diamond windowpanes, Desirée leaned against the dark wainscoting, inspecting one of the plates. She had changed as well, which may have explained when and how Elise had stolen back Rose's birthday dress. Desirée's ebony satin gown was thread-bare and patched. Her face was flushed, her eyes bright and eager. When she saw Rose, she raised a lazy brow and hugged the plate possessively against her chest.

"Sister," she greeted Rose.

Rose stiffened.

"Go to her," Elise whispered, giving Rose's shoulder a gentle squeeze. "Keep the peace as best you can."

Rose licked her lips and headed for Desirée. The two faced each other, dark stepsister, fair daughter.

"I like these plates," Desirée announced.

"They were part of my mother's dowry," Rose replied.

"Well, they're *my* mother's now." Desirée's mouth twisted. "All this belongs to her."

Rose's stomach lurched. Her face tingled and her hands trembled. Then she caught sight of Elise, who was directing a servant to fill a plate and remembered what she had said.

"We had better dishes than these," Desirée continued, raising her chin as if she were challenging Rose to say otherwise. "Our estate was much grander. It was at least twice as big as this one. We had a moat. There were swans in it."

Rose swallowed hard. "You must have been sad to leave it. To come here."

The haughtiness faded from Desirée's face. She looked out the leaded panes at the summer sky. Her shoulders rounded and she was silent for a time.

"There was a fire." Her arms closed around the plate so hard that she would have broken it if it were made of anything but gold. "Stupid Gypsies."

"Oh," Rose managed. Her voice cracked. When Desirée said nothing more, she ventured, "And so . . . ?"

"And so it was destroyed. All of it. Even my clothes," Desirée snapped, wheeling around and glaring at Rose. "And now we're *here*."

Rose remained silent. She didn't know what to say.

As the pause lengthened, streaks of color swept across Desirée's hollow cheeks and high forehead. She took a step back from Rose. Her heel knocked the wall like a hollow laugh.

"We're here," she repeated. Her voice was a little less sure. "And we're not leaving."

She turned back to the window. Rose stayed where she was.

"Go away," Desirée muttered.

Rose took a step backward, glancing around for Elise, when the nurse rushed up behind her and gripped her hand. Her fist against her mouth, she wordlessly shepherded Rose through the room. Ombrine was deep in conversation—with another male neighbor—and didn't notice as the two left.

Elise sped down the hallway and rushed into the music room. Rose's golden birthday harp stood in the center of the room and Celestine's lute lay on an ebony table. On the wall, the portrait of a young woman holding a cat gazed down on them with a smile painted on her pink lips.

"Child, oh, child," Elise said as she looked out into the hall. She shut the doors. Then she took a deep breath and calmed herself as she put her arms around Rose. Rose could feel her heart thundering.

"*Ma belle, ma pauvre,*" she murmured. She took another breath. "Rose, Monsieur Valmont has been arrested."

"*What?*"

"For theft. The plates. The ones he took to pay your father's debts." Elise was shaking. "As soon as she got here, she ordered an inventory of all your father's possessions. She saw them missing and someone told."

"But he took them to save us," Rose insisted. "We'll explain. We'll set him free."

"*Oui,*" Elise said. "We'll save him."

FOUR

A week later, in a trial lasting two hours, Monsieur Valmont was found guilty of theft. He had no records to prove that he had acted in order to satisfy his master's debts and neither Elise nor Rose was allowed to speak on his behalf.

Laurent's creditors realized that if they denied that Valmont had paid them, they could be paid again. Ombrine had the legal right to loosen the Marchand purse strings. So to a man, they lied—save for one honest graybeard. He described to the court how Valmont had struggled to keep the estate running despite the prolonged absence of his master.

"I asked him to pay me only because my own lands have fallen on hard times, and I needed the coin," he announced. "One assumes that . . . *others* pressed him as well and that he took the plates only after his life savings had run dry."

As a result of the man's testimony, Monsieur Valmont's sentence of death was commuted to a life of hard labor in the colonies.

"Imagine, stealing my dress," Desirée sniffed on the night of his sentencing, as she, Ombrine, and

Rose sat at table in the great hall. Their first course was rich *pâté*. Rose wasn't used to dining so formally. She and her mother used to eat with Elise and play a game of cards with her after. Now Elise was banished to eat with the servants. The nurse had begged Rose not to reveal that she'd been the one to take the dress. The truth would do Monsieur Valmont no good, but it would do her a lot of harm indeed. So together they had wrapped it in tissue and muslin and laid it in an old chest, hiding it behind some old furniture beneath the attic eaves. It lay there now.

She had hidden her father's cloak as well, in her sewing basket beneath her bed.

"It was your stepsister's dress and it was ruined anyway," Ombrine reminded her, placing a tiny morsel of venison on her fork. "No matter. Laurent's ships are on their way and they're bulging with goods. I'll have twenty dresses made for you."

"In pink," Desirée insisted, reaching for her wine. "Grander than that other one. Rose's dress was truly not that special. It needed more flounces and bows."

"In black. And tastefully understated. Until our period of mourning is complete." She smiled joyfully at her daughter. "Providence sent Laurent to me."

"*Oui.* Thank the gods he had a heart attack so close to our house," Desirée replied.

Rose ate silently, fuming at their insensitivity. She had threaded their story together. Ombrine's first husband, Louis Severine, had been a wealthy man who lived an ostentatious life. Château Severine was a showpiece and Ombrine constantly redecorated it, adding rooms, and ordering new furniture. They had parties all the time and Ombrine and Desirée were the most sought-after hostesses in the region. Ombrine's wardrobe was legendary. She socialized on a grand scale and Desirée had so many friends she had to keep a list.

Louis was a friendly sort as well. He was very fond of the local Gypsies and gave them permission to camp on his lands. It was said that he was fonder of their women than their men—a rumor Ombrine pretended she had never heard.

One night, a Gypsy husband discovered that his pretty wife was missing and he drank himself into a rage. He and his friends demanded entry into Louis's *château* to search for the lady. Louis refused.

Drunken and furious, the Gypsies melted into the night. They returned three hours later with every man in their clan above the age of thirteen. Each carried a bottle of wine and a torch.

They set Louis Severine's entire estate on fire. The disaster overwhelmed him financially, and Ombrine and Desirée, who had been used to the best of everything, were left penniless. Then he died— some say he drank himself into the grave. His widow and daughter lived in the ruins of the *château* like wraiths and no one came to call. Not one friend stuck by Desirée and all Ombrine's wealthy acquaintances deserted her. Daughter and mother became all the other had and their hearts hardened at the lack of sympathy and friendship. It was no use to count on love and affection. From that time on, they would put their trust in the power of wealth.

And so Ombrine coveted nothing but wealth. She treated the glittering treasures of the Marchand fortune as if they were loaves of bread and she and Desirée were starving. Ombrine spent hours making inventories of all Laurent's possessions—now hers. She hired jewelers and appraisers to put a value on every single object. If so much as a saucer went missing, she knew of it and fined the household staff its stated value against their wages.

Now at the table, Rose sat quietly. She wondered what Monsieur Valmont was having for dinner.

"Eat your venison," Ombrine ordered Rose. "The meat is fresh and succulent."

Rose never ate venison. Artemis favored deer and she was Rose's patroness. Instead Rose took a sip of wine. Her hand trembled around the stem of her goblet.

"Look at her, skin and bones," Desirée sneered. "She eats so little she can barely lift her cup." She picked up her goblet. "And they are very nice cups."

"All the more for us," Ombrine said. She slid a glance at Rose. "Although with her so thin it will be harder to get her married."

"Eat, sister," Desirée sang. "Eat, eat, eat."

Beneath the table, Rose squeezed her left hand into a fist. Her nails drew blood as they dug into her palm. Ombrine and Desirée bewildered her. Their tragedy could explain their greed but not their cruelty. They knew nothing of love, only of loss. She tried to have pity on them.

"The cups are cunning, but these plates are ugly," Desirée announced. "At first I thought they were lovely, but they're awfully garish, aren't they? I think we should finish what that thief Valmont started."

"You may be right," Ombrine declared. "They'd fetch a pretty penny. Honestly, Rose, your mother had terrible taste."

Their hearts were so hardened by their tragedy that they could find no soft spot for someone who had suffered just as much—if not more, for Rose had lost both mother and father.

I pray I will never be so hard-hearted, she thought, glancing down at the blood in her palm.

"*You are loved.*

"*You are loved.*

"*You are loved,*" said the roses in the bower.

Rose lay among them as the statue of the goddess stood watch. It was the night before her fourteenth birthday. In the morning, it would be one year since her mother's death. Almost six months since the death of her father. At moonrise, Rose and Elise had furtively burned incense before her parents' sarcophagi. Weeping, they held each other, a little family of two.

As they passed Ombrine's door, they heard chanting. Rose looked questioningly at Elise. "Perhaps she is celebrating," Elise muttered as she led Rose into her own room. She trailed her fingers down Rose's cheek. "Have a care for the morrow, my girl. She'll cast a shadow on your birthday. Of that I have no doubt."

Rose shuddered. She thought to ask Elise to sleep with her, but her nurse snored dreadfully. She crawled into her bed alone and thought of her mother, and tears spilled down her cheeks.

After Elise fell asleep, Rose crept to the garden. Ombrine had ordered her to stay out of it—especially at night—and promised severe punishment if she disobeyed.

But it was in this garden she had last seen her mother and had heard the joyous news that her father was coming home.

"*You are loved,*" the roses whispered.

"I *was* loved," she said brokenly. "But now they're gone." She began to cry again.

Moonlight gleamed around Rose like her mother's sheltering arms and, after a time, she fell into a deep, heavy sleep.

And in that sleep, a glowing hand cupped a shimmering white mouth pressed against her ear.

A voice whispered, "*Alas, daughter of she who made the wish, you still must walk through the shadows until you see the light. Once you learn the lesson, two broken hearts shall mend.*"

Rose slumbered and didn't hear the voice.

But her heart heard it.

"*You are loved,*" the roses whispered as Rose woke with a start.

Above the statue of Artemis, dawn streaked the sky with washes of lavender and pink. Rose bolted upright with a moan. She'd fallen asleep in the garden and Ombrine would have her head.

A deer had been drinking at the stream. Startled, it darted into the bracken.

Rose touched her cheeks. Her fingertips came back muddy. She hurried to the stream and examined her reflection. Her nose and forehead were filthy too.

"Oh, Artemis, please protect me now," she murmured as she gathered up her skirts. "She'll be so angry."

She raced out of the rose garden, past the two statues of deer, through the hedge maze and the topiary garden, and pushed open the *château's* front door.

Desirée barred her way.

"She's here, Mother!" she cried.

Like a shadow moving across the wall, Ombrine appeared on the stairway. She glided slowly like a wolf.

"She was out all night again," Desirée said triumphantly, her eyes glittering as she stepped out of her mother's way.

"Rose!" came a voice. It was Elise, her long gray braid hanging over her right shoulder of her nightgown, her eyes puffy with sleep. "Child!"

"She is not a child. She is fourteen years old this very day," Ombrine said. Her eyes became slits as she took in Rose's disheveled appearance. "We have gone through this, Rose. There is talk in the village of dark doings. Of groups of sorcerers who gather to do unspeakable things. The wife of the crown prince has died and the baby with her. It is said that magicians were involved."

Rose blinked. Oh, the poor princess. And her little baby too? *Hélas*, what a terrible pity.

"I've heard talk of magic as well," Elise put in. "The prince must be so grief-stricken."

"Alas for him," Desirée said blithely.

"But we are speaking of Rose," Ombrine said, glaring at her stepdaughter.

"*Madame, m'excusez*, but you know I'm not a sorceress," Rose said, knowing she must defend herself. "I did nothing to the princess." In fact, she had lit a candle for Princess Lucienne the very night of her father's death.

Ombrine raised a hand to silence her. "I may know that, but others don't. And others talk. Your father would have wanted you to marry well. But we can't manage that if you continue to shred your reputation by sleeping unprotected in that wretched garden. How many times have I explained this to you?"

"Dozens," Desirée purred. "She just won't listen to you, Mother."

"*Tais-toi*, Desirée," Ombrine snapped. "Will you cease your endless chatter?"

Desirée sputtered, then fell silent.

"I'm sorry," Rose said, understanding an apology was required and she had to make it sound realistic. "I couldn't sleep."

"Allow me to take her to her room, my lady," Elise said with a curtsy. "I'll have her cleaned up and ready for breakfast in no time."

Elise started down the stairs. Ombrine kept her eyes on Rose as she lifted a staying hand. Elise stopped where she was. Desirée caught her breath and bounced on her heels, as if she'd already guessed what was going to happen next.

"As I mentioned," Ombrine said, "Rose is fourteen. She hardly needs a nurse. And as we have no younger children in this family . . ." She let the sentence trail away, unfinished.

Rose's world collapsed to a tiny circle, and the circle was Elise's face. Her nurse's eyes were enormous, her mouth an O of shock.

"We . . . in this house, they keep the nurses on," Elise said in a strangled voice. "I came with Madame Celestine herself, and the understanding was . . . I . . ." She gripped the banister with white knuckles and stared at Rose.

"Oh, please, Stepmother," Rose blurted, taking a step forward. "Please, don't do this. I was wrong to spend the night in the garden and I'll never do it again. I swear it."

"She's an unnecessary expense," Ombrine insisted.

"No, she's not!" Rose wailed. "She's all I have in this world."

Ombrine pulled in her chin as if she'd been slapped and pressed her bloodred fingernails against her chest.

"My dear, your loyalties are misplaced. Mademoiselle Elise is only a servant. But your stepsister and I are your *family. We* are all you have in this world." She turned her head slightly over her shoulder, as if she couldn't quite be bothered to look Elise in the face.

"Start packing," she ordered her, sweeping back up the stairs.

The shadow she cast on the room below was bitter and cold.

Rose and her nurse said their good-byes in the rose garden, weeping as though each had died. Rose was terrified for the old woman, precisely because she *was* old. If Rose's parents were alive, they would have kept Elise at the *château* until her dying day. To be thrown out in the twilight of her life—it was a shame and a stain on the house of Marchand.

"I *was* loved," Rose wept. "You loved me."

"I still love you, sweeting," Elise said hoarsely. She looped a tendril of hair behind Rose's ear. "Don't fret on my account, *ma petite*. I'll be all right."

"Don't lie to make me feel better," Rose protested. "I can't bear this. Oh, gods, I hate her!" She burst into fresh tears.

"I'm well liked in the village," Elise said, gathering her into her arms again. "Someone will take me in."

"I'll write you every day," Rose promised. "I'll send you letters whenever I can. And I'll ask Ombrine to send me to market with the cook, so I can see you."

"Such a good girl." Elise cupped Rose's chin. "Don't send letters. It will anger her. And don't ask to go to the village. If you can manage it, let her think it's her idea to send you. You see how she is."

Rose's hands shook as she wrapped them around Elise's.

"But she doesn't see how you are and there's her loss. Her world is narrow and dark, like a mountain pass. But yours is a beautiful garden."

But the garden was cut back for the winter. The only roses that grew were the purple ones. The rest were sticks and withered leaves.

"It will be a beautiful garden in the spring," Rose said.

"It is beautiful now," Elise insisted. She leaned into the purple roses and breathed in their scent. Rose knew Elise had never heard the roses speak. Nor had anyone else. They whispered only to the daughter of Celestine. Ombrine was unaware that the purple roses even existed. She knew that Celestine had planted the garden and so she had no desire whatsoever to set foot in it.

"I did this to you." Rose's voice broke. "By being willful and disobedient."

"*Non, non, non, ma Rose,*" Elise said, smoothing away the lines in Rose's forehead. "She would have done it anyway. Don't add this weight to the burden you carry."

"It's so wrong!" Rose looked around. She found a stick on the ground and broke it in two. Then she threw the pieces down and stomped on them. Elise watched quietly.

"Then remember that it's wrong," Elise said. "And when you're a great lady, act with mercy and justice."

Rose sank to the ground and buried her face in her hands. "I shall never be a great lady. Nothing will go right ever again."

Elise stroked her hair. "Your mother said much the same thing when she was your age," she said.

Rose raised her tearstained face. "She did?"

Elise nodded. "She had trials and tribulations of her own. They kept her heart very soft. And that, I believe, is why she was able to love you so very, very much. Those who feel deeply, love deeply."

"I would rather be a block of ice," Rose insisted. "I'm done with feeling. Beyond you, I'll never love another human being."

"I doubt that very much." Elise trailed her fingers down the side of Rose's face and drew her back up to her feet. "Oh, how I wish I could watch you fall in love."

"I shall never fall in love," Rose muttered. "Ever."

Elise smiled very sadly. Then she took a breath. "Rose, there is something I have kept to myself. Something I have not dared to speak of. There are some new plants in the herb garden. I've never seen their like before. I don't know what they're for."

Rose understood at once. "I have never eaten from her hand," Rose reminded her.

"I—I won't be here to protect you any longer," Elise continued. Her voice faltered. "I have begged the goddess to guard you. I've offered my life in exchange for yours." Her eyes filled with tears. "Perhaps this is her answer, sending me away."

"The lady of the moon is our guardian, our

patroness," Rose insisted, horrified. "She would never make such a bargain."

"She does not bargain. She answers prayers," Elise replied. "Perhaps we don't always realize what we have asked for."

"You can't go." Rose gripped her arms around her nurse and buried her face in her bosom. "You can't."

But Elise went. And then, the *château* priest. Next, the cook and the seamstresses and the upstairs maid. Down to the scullery and the stable boy, Ombrine rid herself of Laurent's people. Rose stopped asking why.

She found the strange plants in the garden and learned their scent—bitter and cold. Poisonous. Of a night, she heard Ombrine and Desirée singing a mournful dirge over and over and over. They whispered together. They had secrets that sent roots deep into the *château*, like the invader herbs. Secrets that grew and choked out any hope Rose had of becoming a true family.

"*You are loved,*" the roses promised her.

"I'm not," Rose wept, kneeling before the statue of Artemis. "My mother, my father, and my only friend have been taken from me. Everyone who knew my parents is gone. That *monster* sleeps in my mother's bed. How can I be loved, if such things happen to me?"

"*You are loved,*" the roses insisted.

"Rose!"

It was Desirée. Rose grimaced and wiped away

her tears. Her fingertips came back muddy. *When would she learn to stay clean?*

"Rose!" Desirée called again. Her voice was shrill. "Disaster!"

"What now?" Rose muttered.

She got to her feet and trudged out of the garden. She found Desirée twisting and turning in the hedge maze; the older girl had never been able to figure the way. Rose came up behind her as Desirée fluttered her arms like a trapped bird, screaming her name.

"Here I am," Rose said.

Desirée whirled around and Rose took a startled step backward. Desirée's eyes were wild. She barely looked human. Her face was mottled with weeping.

"Laurent's ships," Desirée said. "Gone! Sunk! We are ruined!"

With a banshee wail, Desirée leaped at her step-sister and grabbed her by the wrist. Then she dragged Rose through the maze toward the *château*, shrieking with each wrong turn, unable or unwilling to allow Rose to calm her down enough to lead her out. It was as if she had gone mad.

"Let me help," Rose insisted.

Somehow they arrived at the front door of the *château*, and Desirée burst inside. Rose tumbled over the threshold behind her.

A divan had been set in the center of the foyer, and Ombrine lay on it with the back of her left hand pressed over her eyes. A sheaf of papers fluttered from her right hand as a weathered man in dusty riding clothes turned and looked at the two girls.

His eyes met hers and Rose saw deep pity there. Frightened, she looked down at the papers. The man bent and picked them up.

Rose reached out her hand for them and, in that moment, Ombrine sat up. Her undressed hair hung in tangles around her shoulders, and it was shot through with gray. She looked as wild-eyed as Desirée.

"Those are mine," she hissed. She grabbed the papers from the man and pressed them against her chest. She glared at Rose. "Your father. Your stupid father! The ships went down!"

"Stepmother, I don't understand," Rose said. She looked from Ombrine to the man. He, at least, seemed possessed of his wits.

He said, "*Mademoiselle*, I'm a messenger. Your lady mother has had a shock. It seems her late husband's business enterprises have sustained a blow."

"A *blow*!" Ombrine shrieked at the man. "Get out of here! Leave at once!"

"I've not been paid," the man said calmly.

"Why should you be, with the news you bring?" Ombrine screamed. "Get out!"

He stretched out his hand and said, "If you please, *madame*. Fair news or foul, I am only the messenger."

"Then steal from a widow and her orphans and be damned!" Ombrine reached into the sleeve of her gown and flung a gold coin at him. It slapped him on the cheek. He caught it in his palm and gave her a curt bow.

As he headed for the door, he said to Rose in a low voice, "Have a care, *mademoiselle.*"

Then he walked out the open door.

Ombrine leaped from the divan and slammed the door shut so hard the doorjamb rattled. She threw herself against the door and said, "We are ruined. Utterly." Then she sank to the floor.

"Stepmother," Rose said, taking one uncertain step toward the distraught woman.

"Don't touch me!" Ombrine screamed. "He has taken his fortune to his grave and you put him there! You miserable, loathsome girl! How I hate you!"

"I didn't," Rose whispered, but no one heard her words.

Including Rose herself.

FIVE

With the deaths of Celestine and Laurent and the loss of the Marchand fortune, the shadow across the *château* lengthened, darkened. Who knew what might have happened if Laurent hadn't driven away Reginer, his firstborn and heir? Perhaps the sensitive artist would have been able to enlighten his father's heart. If Reginer could have loosened Laurent's grip on the things of this world, maybe Laurent would have spent more time with Celestine and Rose. Then Celestine might never have uttered the prayer to Artemis that set tragedy in motion.

As it was, Laurent did send Reginer away and Celestine did make her fatal wish. And now, Rose moved through dark times. She no longer desired to feel pity for such a mean, spiteful woman. She became not so much hard-hearted as careful, for she knew if she showed soft feelings to Ombrine, she would cast them away as proof of Rose's weakness.

The Marchands were in trouble. Men who might have courted the Widow Marchand when she was rich stayed well away. Her daughter and stepdaughter were still too young to marry, and without dowries, they would be too poor to attract rich husbands. Hope was slim that some lovelorn gentleman would cast custom to the wind and marry one of the penniless women.

The estate itself was never meant to turn a profit, but simply to feed and clothe its inhabitants. So there was no income there. With no other way to make money, Ombrine's only recourse was to sell the beautiful things she had inherited. First to go were Celestine's dishes, then Rose's harp. Next, the portrait of the blonde woman with the cat.

"If only we had that pink gown," Ombrine muttered. "It was worth a fortune. I hope Valmont is suffering for his sins."

"If he's still alive." Desirée sniffed.

That night, Rose went to the garden and pondered her next move. Was it time, at last, to give her dress to Ombrine? She'd thought often to hand it over, to ease their wretched circumstances. But that would admit some guilt on her part—for they had assumed Monsieur Valmont had stolen it. And it was the only thing she had to remember happier times.

"You are loved," said the roses.

She was wrong. She had more than the dress; she had the roses. So after many tears and second thoughts, she went to the chest beneath the eaves, pulled away the old furniture, and opened it. She moved the layers of muslin and tissue away.

The dress was as beautiful as ever. Elise had embroidered gold thread around the stain, creating a beautiful rose. That would be the proof that she and Rose had had a hand in taking it.

Tight-throated with grief, Rose carefully tore out the stitches. Bit by bit, the rose disappeared.

Then she went to the herb garden and laid it over the bitter herbs carefully, as if perhaps it had blown there by some miracle. She hoped they would find it before the night dew.

A breeze caught the sleeve and it flapped at her as if bidding her *adieu*. She pressed her fingers to her lips and kissed them.

Adieu, happier times.

With each firm step away from it, she was tempted to turn back. A hundred steps brought a hundred second thoughts. But in her deepest heart, it was done.

Grieving, she hurried to the stable and went into Douce's stall. She buried her face against the little mare's warm side. "Oh, *ma petite*," she whispered, "let's ride far away. Let us go. We have nothing to keep us here."

Except that this was her father's house and her mother's rose garden, and she would be found and she would be punished.

Douce nickered and rubbed her forelocks against Rose's arm. It was like a loving caress, the first one she'd had in months and months.

"I love you, too," Rose told her.

"Where did you hide it?" Ombrine demanded shrilly.

She stomped into the stable with Rose's dress in her arms. Desirée followed closely behind her, looking scandalized.

"What? My dress!" Rose cried, feigning surprise as she stepped from the stall. "So Monsieur Valmont didn't take it? Where has it been?"

Ombrine narrowed her eyes. "Don't think to play games with me, girl. You will always lose."

"I play no games," Rose said, lifting her chin. "I am dead serious in all I do." She knew she shouldn't have said it, but she was so angry. She had given the dress of her own accord and the Severine women did not deserve it. They deserved nothing. Not even her attempts to excuse them because of what they'd endured.

Desirée blinked. "What are you talking about? Where was it?"

"I should whip you within an inch of your life. What else have you kept back?" Ombrine demanded.

"You took an inventory of my possessions," Rose replied. "And you took them all."

"You are so impertinent. I don't know why I bother feeding you." Ombrine whirled on her heel as she spoke. "In my homeland, you'd be driven out for this."

Desirée's eyes were huge as she stared back at her mother. "*I*? But I didn't have it!"

Ombrine huffed. "For the love of the gods, Desirée, not *you*."

"You mean *she* had it? How could she have had it all this time? Valmont confessed."

The rest of their conversation was lost to Rose as she trembled, laying her hand on Douce's back. She was surprised Ombrine *hadn't* whipped her or at least demanded an explanation. But then, why should she bother? She had what she wanted.

Rose laid her head against Douce's side, and wept.

The money for the dress went only so far, however. It was gone practically overnight and the family sank back into desperation. Ombrine Severine Marchand was no stranger to fair-weather friends. When her first fortune disappeared, so did the fashionable women of the region. It was no different in the Forested Land. Knowing just how desperate things were, her neighbors carted off coachloads of Marchand treasures that they'd practically stolen. Rose watched it happen, observed Ombrine ignore her humiliation as she tried to get the best deal she could on each and every treasure. Rose wondered if her mother, who had been so kind and gentle, would have done half as well. Perhaps baser instincts had their place in the world.

One evening, just before moonrise, something tugged at Rose. It was almost as if a ghostly hand wrapped around hers, urging her from her icy room into the icier night.

Outside, snowflakes stung her cheeks. Fog moved along the earth and she thought of the night she had tried to save her father's life.

She followed her instinct to the rose garden and her heart leaped. A small square of white lay at the feet of the statue of Artemis.

She fell to her knees in the snow and grabbed it up. It was a letter. With shaking hands, she opened it. A single gold coin fell onto her lap. She closed her fist around it with a gasp.

> Ma chère *Rose*,
> *I have heard of the terrible events at the* château. *My mistress showed me a small cream pot she purchased from the estate for less than a sou. My heart bleeds for you, my sweet girl. I have put a little money by and I send it now to you. It is for you only. I am certain you understand.*
> Je te baise.
> *Tante Elise*

Rose swallowed hard. She rather doubted Elise had taken the dress when she left and it cut her deeply to think of her toiling like a scullery maid, giving her meager wages away. Tears rolled down her cheeks, crystallizing as they dropped to the earth. Elise, her *tante* Elise, her only family. How she longed to go to her.

I could, she thought. *I could saddle Douce and be gone from here forever.*

But she knew that was not possible. Ombrine would come after her. She would have her whipped, or worse.

She folded the letter into a tiny square. Then she scooped out a hollow beneath the purple rose-bush and buried the letter. A tear hit the back of her hand. She was too afraid to leave a reply, but she longed to let Elise know that she loved her, too.

"You are loved," the purple roses whispered to Rose.

And in that moment, she did something she had done only once before. Murmuring, "Forgive me," she picked one of the purple roses.

She half expected it to protest or groan, but it remained silent. She kissed it and whispered to the petals, "Let her know that my heart is with her. Let her know that she is loved and that I have received the gold coin."

Then she laid the rose at the feet of the marble statue.

"Let her messenger know to take it to her," she asked the goddess. "If Tante Elise sees it, she'll know it's from me."

The next night, when Rose stole into the garden, the purple rose had disappeared. Perhaps a deer had devoured it. Perhaps the wind had carried it away.

Or perhaps the statue of Artemis had shot it through the sky on the point of an arrow, to the village far away.

A fortnight passed, and then a month. No second letter followed the first. One night, sleepless and heartsore, Rose walked the stony terraces of the *château.* She didn't know that her mother had done likewise, for many years.

Then she stopped, and looked.

Far below her on the path, Ombrine and Desirée walked together, cloaked and veiled. Ombrine carried a lantern. Rose thought she saw a third figure trailing behind. It was either a tall, menacing shadow, or it was a trick of the light and her fretful mind. Rose squinted, trying to see if it was really there. Then clouds choked off the moonlight, and all Rose saw was a weak flicker of lantern light. When mother and daughter were revealed once more, they were definitely alone.

Three heartbeats later, a large dark bird cawed as it flew across the white face of the moon.

Ombrine turned her gaze toward the place where Rose stood; startled, Rose darted behind a hedge row. Her heart pounded.

"I thought I saw her," Ombrine whispered. The wind carried her voice to Rose.

"She *would* spy," Desirée hissed.

Ombrine raised her chin as if she were sniffing the air. Her profile was sharp and flinty. At that moment, a zigzag of lightning crackled across the sky. Thunder rumbled; the sky broke open and rain poured down.

"Alors!" Ombrine shouted.

Rose took advantage and raced back inside the *château.* Hastily, she grabbed off her shoes and tiptoed in her stockings around the perimeter of the room, so as not to leave wet footprints. Then she barreled up the stairs to her room and shut the door. She threw herself into bed and pulled the covers up to her chin.

She heard Ombrine and Desirée come inside shortly after. They stomped up the stairs, complaining and arguing. An imperious knock rattled her door.

"Rose?" Ombrine called.

Rose bit her lip. Holding her breath, she lay frozen and afraid.

"She's asleep," Desirée said. "She didn't see us."

"Perhaps," Ombrine replied. "We'll have to watch her."

Rose stayed silent.

"Come, then," Ombrine snapped. "It's late."

"You heard what he said. We need more money to pay the Circle for more power. Maybe you should marry her off."

"She's so thin, who would have her without a dowry?" Ombrine replied. "*Non*. We'll cut expenses again to get the money."

"How? What expenses? We already eat scraps. We wear rags."

"*Silence*. We wore rags before and came into a fortune. We can do it again."

The two moved off. Questions pelted Rose's mind like the raindrops on the leaky roof. What circle did they speak of? Who was "he"? Empty of answers, Rose listened to the rain, and she didn't sleep for the rest of the night.

☙ ☙ ☙

After Ombrine fired most of the help, she passed their chores to Rose, who served the meals and cleared away afterward. She also did much of the cleaning and all of the mending. She was such a hard worker that Ombrine fired even more servants.

Rose's soft hands became rough and her back ached most of the time. She remembered what her nurse had said, and made a promise to Artemis if she was ever in a position to hire people, she would treat them fairly and make their burdens light.

Although Rose heard no more talk of circles, Desirée often spoke of the need for more money . . . and then she would look hard at Rose, as if she would shake more treasures loose from her. It chilled Rose, who worked even harder to make herself irreplaceable as a servant.

Then disaster struck again. A terrible disease moved through the livestock. The cows stopped giving milk, sickened, and died. The pigs, sheep, and lambs dropped dead. Ombrine commanded that no one should speak of it beyond the borders of the estate. When the pig boy suggested that their neighbors might have the same problem and may have found a cure, she had him flogged.

"The other estate holders are waiting like wolves for our downfall," Ombrine said. "We must appear to be strong or they'll take advantage of us again."

On a grim gray afternoon, their last milk cow went the way of the others. Now, at supper, Ombrine, Desirée, and Rose ate in gloomy silence.

Ombrine's gown was patched and unfashionable, and dark circles ringed her eyes. But since Rose acted as her maid, her hair, at least, was beautifully arranged.

Rose had dressed Desirée's hair as well, in a circlet and braids that looped around her ears. She let her own hair hang free, unaware that the rivers of wavy gold accentuated her delicate features and starry midnight-blue eyes. With the many chores heaped on her shoulders, she simply didn't have the energy to spend on her appearance.

Finally Ombrine broke the silence.

"This is all your fault," she flung at Rose.

"All your fault," Desirée hissed, pulling apart a chunk of coarse bread. Even when their animals had been healthy, the Marchands no longer ate like nobility. Sometimes, when sitting down to table, Ombrine would stare down at their peasant fare, cover her face, and sob.

"*Oui*, Stepmother," Rose dutifully answered.

"If your father were alive, he'd know what to do. Two men and two fortunes," Ombrine said, sighing. "And the second loss was so unnecessary."

"A waste," Desirée concurred.

Rose put down her spoon and folded her hands in her lap. She kept her gaze lowered. To look straight at Ombrine was to invite her wrath.

"May I be excused?" she asked. "I'm not hungry."

"More for us," Desirée sang, picking up her spoon and reaching toward Rose's bowl.

"How dare you behave so," Ombrine snapped at

Desirée. "We may have no money, but we are not beggars." She gave Rose a sharp nod. "Leave. Be sure to clear the table after we're finished."

"*Oui,* Stepmother." Rose scooted out of her chair.

"You have mending," Ombrine added. "Quite a bit. You've fallen behind."

"*Oui,* Stepmother, I'll get right to it."

"In your room," Ombrine said pointedly.

Rose clenched her fists but said nothing more as she left the table. Her room was cold and drab, and Ombrine seemed to take special delight in forcing her to stay there as much as possible.

She lit a candle, went to her room, and sat down on her bed beside a mound of threadbare clothes. By the dim, flickering light, she took the first piece off the pile. It was Ombrine's black traveling cloak. The wine stain had been patched over like a bandage on a wound, but Rose still remembered how it had gotten there.

By the time the candle was burned halfway down, she had finished the cloak and moved onto one of Desirée's petticoats. Her eyes were scratchy with fatigue and her shoulders throbbed. She tried not to think of the past, when she had spent long hours embroidering beautiful flowers and patterns just for decoration.

A harsh rap on her door made her jump. On the other side, Ombrine said, "We're going to bed. Clear the table and wash the dishes."

"*Oui,* Stepmother," Rose called.

She draped the petticoat over her arm and took

up her candle. The floorboard creaked as she passed Elise's old room. No one slept there now.

She walked down the stairs to the dining room. Something skittered in the darkness, and Rose guessed it was a mouse. Perhaps it had enjoyed a fine feast off her plate.

Neither Ombrine nor Desirée had lifted a finger to carry anything to the kitchen. Desirée's plate sparkled as though she had licked it clean. Ombrine had finished off the decanter of cheap table wine.

Rose scraped the leavings on her own plate into a dish for the pigs, wondering if there were any survivors in the pen. After she washed and dried the tableware and the cooking pots, she blew out her candle to conserve the wax and left it in the kitchen. By the moonlight, she carried the dish to the pigpen. Grunting shapes moved in the darkness; Rose smiled faintly at the evidence of life. Rather than dump such a pitiful amount of food into the trough, she pushed the bowl through a hole in the fence.

Taking a glance over her shoulder, she stole to the rose garden. Her breath caught as she spied another rectangle of white at the base of the statue of Artemis.

This time there were two coins.

> Ma belle chérie,
> *I received your rose.* Merci, ma belle. *I haven't dared to write you again until now, for I feared it*

would go badly for you if Madame Marchand discovered our correspondence. The villagers speak of her worsening temper. But there is talk of a sickness at the château and I am very worried about you. The coins are for medicine. Use them.

There is a man, known only as the Pretender, who has stepped forward claiming to be the oldest son of King Henri. That he is the son of Queen Isabelle, Henri's first wife. Those who have seen him swear that he could pass as Henri when a young man. He swears that a loyal palace guardsman spirited him away at birth because Henri planned to strangle mother and child and replace Isabelle with his mistress, Marie—Jean-Marc's mother. Isabelle could not be saved and the court was told that she had died in childbirth. The Pretender says not. That she was murdered.

They say that it is only a matter of time before the Pretender raises an army and marches on the Land Beyond. Families are sending their men and boys into hiding so that they will not be forced to fight for either side.

The château stands on the road to castle and it may be that such men, coming upon a house of three women without a male relative . . . I need not go on.

So take the coins and buy medicine and if you must run . . . run.

I pray to the goddess that things will change

*and soon. I never dreamed such a fate would
befall you, and it is so very hard to not to be able
to comfort you. Never forget that you are loved.*
   Ever yours,
   Tante Elise

"*Merci,*" Rose whispered. She folded the letter and
buried it as before. Then she plucked another purple
rose, kissed it, and left it at the feet of the statue.

She put the coins in the apron she wore and hurried back to the pigpen to retrieve the dish. It had
been emptied, which gave her hope that in the morning, they would have a pig or two left.

When she reached the dark kitchen, she found
her flint and relit her candle. The yellow light threw
her silhouette against the kitchen wall. She pumped
a bit of water over the dish, planning to wash it with
the next batch.

As she set it on the counter, a larger, blacker
shadow swallowed up her silhouette. Her scalp
prickled. For a moment she thought it was the menacing figure she had seen that rainy night, walking
along the path with Ombrine and Desirée.

She whirled around, to find Ombrine in the
doorway, a candle in her hand.

The light cast her face in hollows, like a skull. Her
eyes were so black they looked like empty sockets.

"What are you doing?" Her voice was taut as
she advanced on Rose. Menace wafted around her
like a fog.

"I—I went to feed the pigs," Rose said haltingly, taking a step backward.

"You liar," Ombrine said. "I watched you from my window. You went to feed the pigs an hour ago."

Before Rose had a chance to answer—saying what, she had no idea—Ombrine darted forward and wrapped her hand around Rose's upper arm. It was the first time Ombrine had ever touched Rose, and her stepmother's skin was as cold as the dead. She dug her long fingernails into Rose's flesh and the pain shot straight into Rose's fluttering heart.

The coins in her apron clinked together. Ombrine's eyes widened.

"What is this?" she screamed. Her hand dove into Rose's apron and emerged with the coins. "Where did you get this? Have you been stealing money from me?"

"*Non, non!*" Rose cried. She didn't know what to do. "I—I found them. Beside the pig trough."

"Liar!" Ombrine shouted. She reached back her free hand and slapped Rose hard across the face. The sound was like a whip crack, the shock so great that Rose momentarily went blind. No one had ever struck her before.

Stumbling as Ombrine dragged her through the kitchen, Rose flung her hand against the jamb to keep from being knocked against it. Her sight returned and all she saw was Ombrine's square shoulder and tangled hair in a nimbus of candlelight.

They took the stairway, Ombrine practically

running up the stairs as she pulled Rose behind like a recalcitrant donkey. At the landing, Desirée appeared, grinning and excited. She was wearing the purple cloak Rose had been embroidering for her father.

"What are you doing? What is that?" Ombrine demanded, jerking Rose in front, then pushing her again to keep her moving.

"I found it," Desirée said. "It's not worth anything, Mother. It will merely keep out the cold."

"Then give it to me. Everything here is mine, to do with as I wish. Is that not so, Stepdaughter?"

Rose couldn't stop staring at the cloak. Everything about that night rushed in . . . and everything about this one. The world had shifted on its axis again and something even more wicked was on its way.

SIX

The winds blew and the world turned, and before she knew it, Rose was sixteen. She continued to work like a slave and disaster dogged the Marchands at every turn. One night the *château* caught fire and nearly burned to the ground. Ombrine announced that every coin she had saved went to patch the roof and a couple of walls, barely adequate to keep out wild animals and weather. She threatened all the servants with a beating—Rose included—if they so much as whispered about the condition of the *château* with anyone.

And so, Laurent Marchand's beautiful home was gone. His lands were in a shambles. The topiary garden and hedge maze died. If anyone in the Forested Land ever spoke of him, it was to say that his life had been a waste.

Despite the fact that no one tended the beautiful garden Celestine had created, it continued to flourish. The purple rosebush blazed bright as a sunrise below the protective gaze of the goddess Artemis. The magic of undying love sustained it. In the few moments Rose could manage to steal away, the garden sustained her.

But there were no more letters and no more coins. Though she herself was not sent to market, she asked the servant who regularly went to look for Elise. He said no one had heard of her, which made Rose suspect he hadn't asked at all.

Of a night, she heard Ombrine and Desirée walking past her room, down the stairs and out of the *château*. She would listen for their return hours later. They would murmur together about "the circle," and about "him." The strange plants in the herb garden were joined by more, and occasionally she smelled an odd, sulfurous odor emanating from Ombrine's rooms.

She feared witchcraft and she became more cautious, more alert. She prayed to Artemis for protection— and she began to carry a knife in her apron. She made certain she cooked every meal in the *château*, taking nothing from Ombrine's hand. She thought of running away, weaving fantasies of fleeing to the village, locating Elise, and joining Monsieur Valmont in the colonies. Life there would certainly be preferable to life here. But she didn't act; she was certain Ombrine would find them and punish them all severely.

Life had become a matter of survival and it took all Ombrine's resources to keep her people from dying of starvation. She no longer worried about mending and clean sheets. A turnip was as precious as an embroidered cloak.

Although Rose was in more danger of dying then than she had ever been, the disastrous change in circumstances yielded a benefit: freedom. Ombrine didn't care where her stepdaughter roamed—as long as she returned with something for the family to eat. If Rose failed, Ombrine would fly into a rage and hit her.

Thin, bruised, and nut-brown from the sun, Rose would stretch on her back in the rose garden after her days of hard labor, pray to her goddess, and listen to the roses.

"You are loved.

"You are loved.

"You are loved."

She remembered a night long ago when her mother had promised her birthday magic and how that night had been Celestine's last. She remembered how urgently her mother had wanted her to know that she was loved. Starving, destitute, and alone, she wondered why it was so important. Could love feed her? Could love protect her? If she was loved, why was she so close to death herself?

She gazed up at the statue of Artemis and whispered, "Why is all this happening?"

"You are loved," the roses whispered and that was the only reply.

One dry spring afternoon in her sixteenth year, Rose was searching the deep wildwood for mushrooms. The limbs of the trees interlaced, creating canopies that shielded the loamy earth from the sun. Some places in the forest were so dark that she had to search by candlelight. She kept her candle, her flints, and her precious shoes in the bottom of her gathering basket. She had one pair of shoes left, made of splotched and tattered leather. Her rows and rows of lovely velvet slippers had disintegrated long ago.

Her stomach growled with hunger. Her hands trembled. She usually found a treasure of little brown caps, but today, there was nothing and her hands shook harder at the thought of coming back empty-handed. Hunger made for anger and everyone was always hungry, especially Ombrine. It hadn't rained all month, and crops were withering in the fields. The Marchands were lucky; they still had their silvery stream.

The shadow that had fallen over the Marchands was spreading everywhere. The Pretender was massing his troops against the king. War was coming and the estates were hoarding what food they could manage to coax from the ground. Peasants and villagers had to fend for themselves and the pickings were getting slimmer.

She decided to give up the search for the day. She was tired and hungry, and night was beginning to fall. She would stop at the rose garden for some solace and to prepare herself to face Ombrine with an empty basket.

She was back on the grounds sooner than she would have liked. The ruined *château* rose in the gloom like a watchful wolf, eager to run some food to ground.

Shivering, she walked past the statues of the two does, eager to rest for a few moments among the roses and hear that she was loved.

She took one step. Then two. Then Rose threw back her head and let loose a shriek of terrible grief.

Desolation. Utter ruin. Her one sanctuary, demolished.

In the center of the garden, the fountain was still. The statue of Artemis lay smashed into chunks. Her head lay on its right cheek; her marble eyes stared at the carnage. All the rosebushes had been pulled up. They lay in heaps like kindling, their roots exposed, their blossoms curled up and withered. Pinks, crimson, scarlet, orange . . . and purple.

Along with the others, the purple rosebush was dead.

Wailing, Rose shambled forward. Her feet were numb. She couldn't feel her body as she fell to the ground beside the purple bush. She gathered up the papery blossoms and buried her face in them, listening.

Their voices were dead.

She fell into despair, a well of shadows; she plummeted, having no idea that she was digging ruts with her knife as she screamed and wept. She raged until there was nothing left, not a sound, and her fingers sank into the gouges in the dirt. She lay whimpering until a voice clattered over her shattered heart like horse hooves on cobblestones.

"For the love of the gods, Rose, calm down."

Moonlight shone down on Ombrine. Silhouetted by dead rosebushes, she stood at the entrance to the garden in Celestine's wide-brimmed gardening hat tied beneath her chin with a bow. She wore Celestine's leather gardening gloves. Desirée stood beside her in Laurent's cloak.

"We need more space to grow more food," Ombrine said as if Rose had asked why she'd done it. "The other estates are paying high prices for produce and we must take advantage. We have a stream and they don't. We'll sell the excess in the market. It's the only way we can survive."

What is the point? What is the point of surviving? Rose thought. She had left her heart in the dark well, and she gripped the knife. She realized that she thought to use it, whether on herself or Ombrine, she wasn't sure. But she did know that she had reached the end, the bitter end.

Ombrine cleared her throat. Maybe she knew that she had gone too far. Maybe somewhere inside her, a shred of decency railed at her for the wound she had inflicted on another living soul.

If that was the case, Ombrine concealed it. She said impatiently, "Now come along. In the morning, we'll go the village to hire some day laborers. We'll haul everything out and prepare the earth for planting."

Maybe in that moment, a weaker soul *would* have stabbed her through the heart. Or a more foolish soul would have ignored the fact that the odds stood at two to one and the keeper of the knife was famished and exhausted.

Whatever the case, Rose knew she wasn't going to murder Ombrine. But she hadn't ruled out ending her own life. Part of her thrilled at the very thought that she held the power of life and death in her hand, that she could do something, anything, to alter her future.

"Artemis," Rose gasped, calling on her patroness.

"Gravel," Ombrine said. "To save the wagon wheels. There are so many holes in our road. We don't need statues. We need money."

"Come on, Rose," Desirée cut in. Her voice was gleeful and triumphant. "You can't lie there all night."

"Artemis," Rose whispered in a strangled voice, as she pressed her thumb against the edge of the knife. It was very sharp. It would be quick.

"Rose," Desirée mimicked her. "You haven't made dinner and we're hungry."

"Oh, leave her," Ombrine said to her daughter. "More for us."

"More *what?*" Desirée demanded. "Nothing's made!"

"Then you'll make it." Ombrine's voice trailed away.

"I?" Desirée's voice grew fainter as well. *"Cook?"*

Rose lay motionless, staring without seeing. She wasn't certain she was still breathing. She saw herself blending with the earth, joining her parents.

The moon glowed on the ruined garden and the wounded girl. The absence of the water splashing in the fountain was a sound in itself: She was not loved and Rose believed she never would be again. She would die and no one would miss her, except at mealtimes.

She held the knife like the hand of a friend. Perhaps peace was all that she could wish for and that peace would come with the end of her life. Could it be that Ombrine had done this terrible thing to push her to do it? Was she truly that evil?

She didn't have the spirit to cry or even to blink. As she gripped the knife, the breeze kissed her cheek like the memory of one who had loved her. Her eyelids grew heavy and she fell into a deep sleep.

While she slept, the memory of her mother's wish wafted on the night breeze. The moonlight gathered up Celestine's hopes, planted so long ago in the garden of her daughter's heart.

> *"Let her know that she is loved with a love that is true and will never fade as the rose petal fades. If she knows that, it will be all that she needs in this life. A woman who is loved is the richest woman on earth. Knowing you are loved is the safest of harbors. True love never dies. It lives beyond the grave, in the heart of the beloved. If she knows she is loved, she'll be rich and safe for all her days."*

The head of the statue of Artemis lay on the earth. Tears welled and spilled because the goddess was bound to answer the prayers of those who belonged to her. And Celestine Marchand had been her Best Beloved. Thus, she had no choice but to fulfill her dying wish.

Although the journey Artemis had sent Rose on was not the journey she might have chosen for her had she the power, she knew it was a good one—if Rose had the heart to complete it. She didn't know if Celestine's Best Beloved would walk through the valley of the shadow into the light or if she would falter and remain there. It was not up to the gods. It was up to Rose. And so, for Rose's sake—and because it was in Artemis's nature to protect women—she wept for the girl and did what she could to send her some strength.

From the wildwood just past the silvery stream, a perfect little doe crept toward the sleeping girl. As she drew nearer, her fur turned white, and her eyes, dark blue. When she touched Rose's limp hand, she turned into a luminous being . . .

. . . holding out a purple rose.

> *"You took it from me once, and started your journey. You may stop here. You may rest. You may die if you wish. Or you may go on. If you stop, you stop in shadow. The light awaits you, daughter of Celestine, but to reach it, you will be transformed. You will be changed. You will not be as you are now. Know that before you make your choice.*
>
> *"Know too, it is your choice to make."*

And then the being became a brown doe again, with a purple rose in her mouth. She dropped it to the earth like a votive offering.

"*You are loved,*" it whispered to Rose.

In the Land Beyond . . .

"*Mon amour,*" Jean-Marc murmured, his whisper an echo in the mausoleum beneath the temple to Zeus.

His heavy gold crown clanked against the stones as he set it down and knelt beside the sarcophagus of his wife. Her effigy lay in repose and he traced her profile with his lonely gaze. Though her marble features were unpainted, he could still see the exact color of her eyes—starry midnight blue—and her hair, lustrous as newly minted gold coins.

If he closed his eyes, he could smell her dainty attar of roses, and hear her voice whispering his name. Whispering, "*I am so sorry, I am sorry,*" as she died, taking their young son with them. "*I promised you I wouldn't leave, but the gods have willed it otherwise.*"

He felt tricked and betrayed. His son—Espere—had been born but he had not lived.

And the king's heart was broken beyond mending.

At Jean-Marc's command, his infant son's effigy had not been included on the sarcophagus, although Espere's bones lay with his mother's. The symbol of his short life was the stone rose between Lucienne's hands, sheltered gently there with a mother's love.

"Gods, ease my pain," he moaned, bending his fingers into a double fist and resting his forehead on them. "For the sake of my kingdom, kill all feeling in me. Let me forget what love is like. Then I will do what must be done."

Heavyhearted, he pulled a deep, bloodred rose from his tunic and lay it atop the stone one. Sweets for the sweet. Weeping, he bent over her and kissed the marble lips.

"I *must* marry," he said brokenly. "But I will never love again. This I swear to you, queen of my heart." He touched the stone rose. "Espere, my son, my child, watch over your lady mother. Keep her well until we are reunited again."

How could a heart so shattered with grief break again, and yet again? But it happened, as Jean-Marc sobbed for his family and all that had been taken from him, again and again.

At last, King Jean-Marc straightened, took up his torch, and walked up the stairs as the deep gong signaling the dawn rattled his spine. He squared his shoulders and lifted his chin. He walked out into the courtyard where his guards waited. They straightened at his approach.

In time, it will not hurt so much, he promised himself, *and I won't care who shares my throne.* But men lied, the same as gods did.

When he emerged from the temple, dawn was blossoming across the cloak of night. He heard the drumming of the threshers and the blare of a hunting horn, and groaned. He had promised his nobles a hunt this morning. He had no desire to mix with them or to mix with anybody. But he knew he had to keep them close—or to at least give the illusion of doing so.

He said to the bodyguards, "We'll go to the stables."

An hour later, Jean-Marc's fiery steed La Magnifique cantered to the rhythm of the beaters as they marched ahead on foot through the stands of parched chestnut trees. They pounded the large drums tied to their waists, flushing out the game with their frightening thunder. The birders bore hooded kestrels on their leather gauntlets, and the bells on the birds' leather caps jingled in unison with La Magnifique's pounding hoofbeats. Dressed in a black leather jerkin, Jean-Marc wore a quiver of arrows and his longbow was tied by a thong to his saddle.

The hounds bayed and bounded ahead, on the scent. Jean-Marc's courtiers surrounded him on horseback, the gentlemen in jewel-toned velvets and leather, the ladies riding sidesaddle, coquettishly showing the lace of their petticoats. The hunting party was in high spirits—after all, they were riding with the king—and Jean-Marc found himself feeling like an outsider, as he had in all his days before he had married Lucienne. What joy could they find? Did they notice the desperate straits of the forest and her creatures? The trees were tinderboxes waiting to burn. The animals were so thirsty they might very well wish they were dead.

He put his spurs to La Magnifique and galloped ahead of the others. He was suddenly seized with the mad thought that he would ride away, flying past the borders of his kingdom and into some new, unmarked territory where no one else could follow. Before he had married Lucienne, that place had been his heart.

The horse ran so hard that his hoofs hardly touched the dusty earth. He whinnied with joy, and Jean-Marc loosened the reins, giving him his head. They were a blur, man and horse, and he supposed his guards were about to throw themselves on their swords because they couldn't keep up with him.

La Magnifique cleared a dry streambed, then they approached a sharp incline that the steed swooped over like an eagle. Ahead, the suffering woods were dark and deep, and Jean-Marc supposed they should slow down, or preferably turn back. But the thought was as bitter as poison.

Still, his conscience got the better of him. He had a duty not to break his neck. Reluctantly, he gathered up the reins and prepared to slow La Magnifique down. The horse would be just as disappointed as his owner but his next chance to run flat out would come much sooner than Jean-Marc's.

Jean-Marc clicked his tongue against his teeth, a signal to the beautifully trained mount that the wild run was over. La Magnifique chuffed as if to protest but he pulled himself in and slowed as they reached a small clearing.

And then he saw her.

Across the crackled meadow, a velvet-brown doe raised her delicate head and stared straight at him. She was perfectly formed. He'd never seen such an exquisite deer. What a trophy she would make. Swiftly he unhooked his bow from his saddle and slid an arrow from the quiver. He notched it and took aim.

The doe's gaze didn't waiver. Intelligence blazed in her eyes and there was a serenity in her bearing. She was aware of him and yet unafraid.

Moved, he lowered his bow. Far be it for him to end the life of such a creature. He unnotched the arrow and replaced it in the quiver.

The doe walked toward him. As Jean-Marc looked on, the doe blazed with light; she became pure white, shimmering like a fallen star. Her eyes turned midnight blue. Then she transformed into a human shape.

Jean-Marc immediately dismounted and knelt on the ground, his head lowered. He knew that he was in the presence of a god.

"Not a god," a breeze whispered against his ear. *"A messenger. You have spared the servant of the Goddess of the Hunt and of the Moon."*

"Artemis," Jean-Marc murmured. His heart skipped beats. Anger mixed with his awe. Artemis had been the patroness of Lucienne but the goddess had not protected her handmaiden.

"Know this: You must have hope. You will love again."

Never, Jean-Marc thought, keeping his head bowed so that the being wouldn't see the fury and despair in his face.

At that precise moment, something slammed

down on top of him with a rib-breaking crack and ground him face-first into the ground. Fingers clutched his hair and jerked his head backward.

A voice shouted, "Death to the usurper!" and Jean-Marc felt the keen press of a blade beneath his chin.

Then his attacker jerked, groaned, and crumpled sideways on the ground. Immediately Jean-Marc rolled out from beneath him and prepared to spring.

An arrow stuck out from the back of the man's neck. The man's mouth worked, the bloody foam burbled out of his mouth, and he died.

"Your Majesty!" someone called.

It was his chief bodyguard, his bow in his hand. He was still riding his horse, and his face was gray with terror. Jean-Marc held up his hand to show that he was all right. But the truth was, he thought he'd broken a rib.

"Thank the gods," the bodyguard said as he pulled up beside his king.

"*À cause de toi*," Jean-Marc replied. *Thanks to you.*

Jean-Marc looked down at the assassin, wondering if the goddess had sent him. How else could he have known the king would ride into the forest? Had someone informed the Pretender of Jean-Marc's great hunt?

The rest of the hunting party sped to a halt, gawking at the dead man and rejoicing that His Majesty was all right. Several of the women acted as if they were about to collapse, it was all so upsetting.

Better that they lose their own lives than their handsome, young, available monarch lose his. . . .

In a low voice, Jean-Marc said to the bodyguard, "I don't think I can ride. I need a litter." He knew he had to take care. He had brought this misfortune on himself; he couldn't bring tragedy to the country by puncturing a lung with the jagged end of a broken rib.

"A litter for the king!" the bodyguard bellowed. He said to Jean-Marc, "The court painter lives near here, sire. We can take you to his *château.*"

"Very well," Jean-Marc grunted. Then he closed his eyes and tried to will away the pain.

Something whispered, *"You will love."*

And it began to rain.

SEVEN

Raindrops woke Rose. She felt strangely peaceful. Then she gazed down at the rose draped over her hand. She caught her breath and looked around for the one who had left it for her.

A luminous being knelt beside her. It had been watching her sleep.

"*You are loved,*" the rose whispered to her.

"Oh, *merci,*" Rose said to the being. It pointed at the statue.

"*À cause d'Artemis,*" it told her. "*I am but her messenger. You have a choice to make.*"

"I—I remember my dream," Rose replied, her voice shaking.

It hefted its bow in its arm and drew an arrow from the quiver. "*Shall I shoot?*" It notched the arrow and pointed it directly at her.

Rose took a deep breath. She understood that she was at a crossroads. She knew she could give up and it would be all over.

The being waited.

The rose whispered, "*You are loved.*"

Rose shook her head. She lifted her chin and said, "I will go on."

"*So are heroes born,*" the being said with approval. Then, without warning, it vanished in an instant and she was alone.

"Rose!" Ombrine bellowed from the entrance to the garden. She was wearing Celestine's gardening hat and gloves. Beside her, Desirée was huddled under an umbrella, wrapped in Laurent's cloak. "*Allons-y!* We're going to the village!"

"In the rain?" Desirée cried.

"Our produce will rot if we do not," Ombrine said. She huffed. "This rain. If the drought ends, our prices will go down."

"I don't want to go." Desirée pouted. "It's too cold."

Rose couldn't help her smile. This was her reward for agreeing not to die. She had never been taken to the village since her nurse had been exiled. *Tante Elise,* she thought joyfully. *I'll find her at last.*

"*Allons-y!*" Ombrine repeated impatiently. "Let's go!"

"*Oui,* Stepmother," Rose said, feigning calm. But inside her pockets, her hands trembled, and she stroked the rose gently like a fragile talisman.

The Marchands had long ago traded their fine coach for a wagon, pulled by a dray horse and dainty little Douce, who seemed very out of place in front of such a humble conveyance, but pulled and tugged as best she could. Ombrine, Rose, and Desirée piled in.

The hood of her black traveling cloak thrown over her head, Ombrine took up the reins. As they bumped along past the scarecrow and the little shrine, Rose remembered the night she had taken the fork in the road to the mountains. What a brave, impetuous thing that had been to do. She was still that girl.

By the time they reached the village, the rain had stopped and Apollo's chariot warmed the gray sky. The wooden buildings were splintered and muddy. A faded sign wagged in the wind. There were no men about. All had gone for soldiers, and the village was run by women who had too many burdens already. Despite the promise of wages to come, no one could be hired to help Ombrine put in her new vegetable garden.

"There must be someone somewhere," Ombrine grumbled. "Search around," she snapped at Rose. She'd not spared a moment of gratitude for the end of the drought.

Rose curtsied to her stepmother and ran as fast as she could to the tavern. In her pocket, she protectively held the tiny purple rosebud, whose soft petals seemed to caress her fingertips. Perhaps she could persuade Ombrine to hire Elise to put in the garden. At the thought, she picked up her pace, dashing like a madwoman down the slippery streets.

At the tavern, which was empty of patrons and very cold, she found an old woman huddled by a single bubbling pot of stew in the fireplace. She was wrapped in a shabby gray shawl and woolen cap.

Rose asked, "*S'il vous plaît, madame,* please tell me where Elise Lune is? The old lady who cleans the stables?" she added as the grizzled woman gazed at her with a strange look. Then she cackled as if something greatly amused her.

"Out back," she told Rose.

"*Merci, madame,*" Rose said, curtsying. She ran through the tavern and burst through the back door, crying, "Elise! *C'est moi, Rose!*"

And then she realized why the old woman had laughed: A peasants' graveyard lay before her, with perhaps four dozen graves. There were few markers of any sort and most of them were wood. One was newer than the others. ELISE LUNE had been cut into the wooden face, the letters painted in white. There were dates.

Her sweet old nurse had died a year and a month before and she was put in the earth with a stone to tell her name and little else. There was no mention of the nights she had cradled Rose as a teething infant, or clapped her hands when Rose took her first steps, or sat with her young lady after the death of Celestine.

On the mound of the grave, a purple rosebush grew. Two lush, purple roses rested among the thorns and leaves: The two roses Rose had sent her must have taken root.

"No, oh, by the gods, no," Rose sobbed. She fell to her knees, pressed her face against the mound and whispered, "I love you, Elise, you cannot be dead!"

The purple rose she had brought with her tumbled

out of her pocket. It landed on the grassy dirt, and joined their chorus. "*You are loved.*"

She wept, and then wept harder. Her tears flooded the earth. If it had not already rained, her grief would have ended the drought.

"*You are loved,*" the roses vowed.

And as she sobbed, she thought perhaps the goddess had tricked her into agreeing not to die because she had suspected the death of Elise would be too much to bear. Because it was.

It was.

And yet . . . she bore it. The pain was physical, it was unbelievable. It was the final crack in her broken heart.

And yet . . . she still knew she was loved.

"And *I* love. I love Elise, and I love my parents, and I love my goddess." She reached forward to touch the roses.

The earth shifted again and the scales rebalanced.

She was sixteen and she had just grown up.

"I'll come back and tend you," she promised the roses. They seemed to turn their faces to her. They seemed to understand that this was where the garden would be next. "I'll bring the garden here and no one will take it from me . . . or from anyone who comes here to mourn their losses."

Wiping her face, she kissed each rose, then put her arms around the gravestone and hugged it tightly, weeping. "I will move forward, Tante Elise," she said. "I will keep you alive in my heart. I swear it."

Those who love feel deeply, and Rose felt great, great grief. But grief was not the same as utter despair.

Not at all.

Grief was power and it filled her with resolve.

"Where have you been gadding?" Ombrine demanded when Rose had returned to the village square. Rose's stepmother was pacing back and forth behind the empty wagon. All their vegetables had been sold—a triumph!—but Ombrine made no mention of it.

Desirée was sitting on the wagon seat, examining something inside a black leather pouch. When she looked up and saw Rose, she closed the drawstrings tight and put the pouch in her pocket.

"I've been looking for laborers," Rose lied.

Ombrine balled her fists. "And I see you failed. Gods! There is no one. No one!"

"No matter, Stepmother," Rose assured her. She had formulated a plan. "I'll put the garden in myself. I'll tend the vegetables and I'll harvest them. Alone. All I ask in return is that I may come to the village when you sell them."

"Alone?" Desirée said. She raised a brow. "You can hardly walk."

"No matter." Rose squared her shoulders. "I'll do it, if I may come to the village."

"You dare to bargain with me?" Ombrine asked.

"Why not? *We* make bargains," Desirée answered with a sly, knowing smile.

"*Tais-toi,*" Ombrine snapped at Desirée. Her

cheeks flushed. "You're up to something," she declared, but Rose could see that she was past worrying about what that might be. "You'll have to load and unload the wagon as well."

"*Oui*, Stepmother," Rose answered with a curtsy.

And they went home.

As she had bargained, Rose planted a new garden in the enchanted fairy bower of her childhood. Her workroughened hands were blistered as she dug the rows and turned the earth; her back never stopped aching, as she put in beans and lettuces and turnips. As with Celestine's rose garden, the seeds exploded and bloomed into a profusion of vegetables, so perfect and plentiful that soon they were the talk of the village. Ombrine didn't give Rose any credit for the luxurious yield. The dirt was rich there, she claimed. It was obvious: Hadn't the rose garden flourished as well?

But Desirée said, "Always give credit where it is due, Mother, or *someone* might get angry."

"Hush." Ombrine glared at Desirée. "You are unbelievably reckless and foolhardy." Then to Rose she said, "You've done well." She glared at her daughter again, as if in warning.

Rose had no illusions that Desirée had meant that she deserved the credit. Her stepfamily was quarreling about a different matter altogether. She cast down her eyes, picturing the strange herbs in the garden and the shadow she thought she had seen so long ago. They were still up to something, still in league with shadows. She remembered Ombrine's talk of sorcerers in the land, and an icy finger of dread tapped against her backbone.

Ombrine, Rose, and Desirée went to market once a week, and the masters of the neighboring estates sent their cooks to lay claim on the Marchand bounty as soon as the wagon wheels clattered into the town square.

Each trip, Rose stole away to Elise's grave. The roses had grown into three large bushes, which sent out shoots to the neighboring graves. The mounds of the dead were wild with color. As she pruned them and fed them and checked them for parasites, Rose would sit and talk aloud as if Elise were still alive, and the purple roses would murmur to her that she was loved. The garden was magnificent and Rose knew that love made it grow. Seeing the glorious evidence that love could not die, she dared to hope that someday, another living person would love her.

One market day, as she sat beside the grave, a shadow fell across the rosebush and she looked up, startled. A tall blond man towered over her and he took a step backward when he looked at her. He was much older than she and dressed in the black-and-gold livery of the king. There was something about the smile lines around his eyes that made her unafraid of him and she smiled at him in turn.

When their gazes locked, his eyes widened, and he swept a courtly bow. Rose was amused by his gallantry; she sat in tatters and rags, and he was clearly a gentleman, above her in every way. She got to her feet and curtsied.

"*Bonjour, monsieur*," she said politely.

"*Bonjour*," he replied. "I'm sorry. I didn't mean to intrude on your privacy. I saw those roses from the road, and I had to take a closer look. I've never seen anything like them."

"*Non, monsieur*," she replied. "I expect you haven't."

Together they looked at the flowers. Their purple hue was vibrant and alive. Rose watched to see if he could hear their whispers but he gave no indication.

"Might I buy one?"

"*Oui*." Rose was astonished at herself. The word had sprung from her lips, although she had had no plan to say yes. Then, because she had never sold one of the roses and didn't want to now, she named an outrageous price.

"Done," he said.

Rose was dizzy. She had not seen that much money in years. What could she do with such a sum? What would she do? Was this a way to buy her freedom?

He reached into a leather pouch at his waist and counted out the coins, then paused and said, "Might I buy a dozen?"

On the ride back to the *château* from the village, after Rose had sold the purple roses to the gentleman, she was taken ill with a fever. Overheated and sick to her stomach, she hid the fortune the blond man had paid her for her roses in a leather pouch under her mattress, and lay in bed all week. Ombrine was disgusted with her and threatened her with a beating if she didn't pull herself together. But Rose took two steps from her bed and crumpled in a heap on the floor.

"We'll go without you," Ombrine announced. Soon after, Ombrine and Desirée left and Rose was alone. For long hours she languished in her sickbed. Her lips were chapped, her throat parched. She remembered her mother's sweet voice, singing to her when she was ill. She could almost feel Elise's cool hand on her forehead, sponging away the heat.

She woke up to their voices, followed by a sharp knock on the door. It opened before she could speak. As she sat up in her bed, Ombrine glided toward her with a candle in her hand, and there was something odd about her eyes. In the flickering light, they appeared completely black. Rose drew back with a gasp.

"What is it, Rose? Did I startle you?" Ombrine's voice was a little shrill, a little wild, as if she had been drinking.

"I was asleep," Rose managed. Her heart skipped beats. "How was it at the market?"

"The market? Oh!" Ombrine smiled. "We did well." She reached forward and pressed her fingertips against Rose's forehead. "You're still feverish," she said. "I'll bring you a brew. Tomorrow you'll get back to work, *oui*? There's no rest for the wicked."

Her smile grew. Her teeth seemed sharper than

usual and Rose tried very hard not to betray her alarm. Whatever Ombrine brewed, she would never drink it.

Ombrine turned and walked toward the door. Her shadow grew and grew, thrown against the wall like a mountain. Two tiny horns sprouted from the shadow's head. Rose looked at Ombrine, and saw nothing but her hair piled atop her head.

I'm seeing things because I'm sick. Rose closed her eyes, but her heart was beating so fast she was afraid she might die.

A short time later, Ombrine stood in the doorway with a goblet between her hands. Steam rose from the bowl as she glided forward.

"Here, Rose," she said in a lilting tone. "Here is something to make you feel better."

Rose licked her lips as she regarded the steaming goblet. A terrible odor rose from it and she knew she would rather die of fever than put her lips to the rim. Remembering the first time Ombrine had offered her a cup of wine, she took it. As she lifted it to her mouth, she feigned a cough and let go of the goblet. It tumbled end over end and landed on the floor.

"You clumsy idiot!" Ombrine shrieked.

Rose coughed again as she slid from beneath the covers and began to mop up the wine with her ragged bedsheet. The smell was so strong that her eyes began to water.

"I'm so sorry, Stepmother," Rose said contritely.

Ombrine huffed. "Clean it all up." Then she turned

on her heel and stomped out of the room, slamming the door so hard that she shook the plaster from the wall.

Once she was done, Rose carried the sodden sheet across the room, thinking to rinse it in the kitchen. But Ombrine had locked her in.

Rose trembled. The axis of the earth had shifted once more. She could feel it, feel the imbalance and the wrongness. Something had changed. Something was coming.

She dropped the sheet beside the door.

Then she went to check her money bag, hidden beneath her mattress.

She gasped.

It was gone.

Rose searched her entire room for her money. Someone had taken it while she'd lain asleep or in a faint. She paced, ill, half-delirious, outraged, and frightened. And yet, strangely hopeful. She had a way to bring in money now and Ombrine knew it. Perhaps at last her stepmother would value her. Even be kind to her.

But Ombrine brought her no more potions. Nor did she bring her food. She completely ignored her. That was not what Rose would have expected.

And yet, one morning, she found that the door was unlocked and felt well enough to go downstairs and forage in the larder. As she took the stairs slowly and carefully, she found Ombrine and Desirée eating breakfast and the smell of food made her stomach rumble.

Desirée said, "Thank the gods you're up! I swear I couldn't cook another meal." She grimaced at her plate of runny eggs and pushed it away. Rose was so hungry she had to force herself not to dart forward and grab it.

"I'm glad to see you've recovered," Ombrine told her, but irritation and frustration rose off her in waves. Ombrine wasn't glad. She sat in stony silence while Rose seated herself and began nibbling at a piece of cheese and a bit of bread.

"One needs a plate and cutlery," Ombrine said tightly. "Unless one is a peasant."

Rose was too dizzy to move, so she swallowed down the last of the bread and cheese.

"Well, then, we see what she is," Desirée declared.

Ombrine pushed back her chair.

"Clean up," she said as she swept out of the room.

After Rose had cleared and washed the dishes, Ombrine glided into the kitchen with Rose's gathering basket against her chest. She held it out to her and said, "We're quite low on food. Go out into the woods and see what you can find. Some mushrooms, perhaps. Or berries."

As Rose took the basket, her fingers brushed against her stepmother's stone-cold hand. In her mind's eye, the forest shadows slithered together, forming the dark silhouette of a man. His eyes glowed red and he carried a knife.

A knife meant for her.

"Rose?" Ombrine snapped.

"*Oui*, Stepmother," Rose managed, with a curtsy.

She began trembling from head to toe. Was she seeing her own future? Was it a warning?

"Don't come back until you have found something," Ombrine told her.

"*Oui*, Stepmother," Rose said again.

Shaking, she walked out of the *château* as calmly as she could. Then she ran to the stable to hop on Douce and gallop to the village. Or past the village. To leave the Forested Land, and find somewhere safe.

But Ombrine's stable boy was there, mucking out the stable of the dray mare. He gazed up at Rose through the grime on his face, then leaned saucily on his pitchfork as he looked her up and down.

As steadily as she could manage it, she walked past him to Douce's stall. It was empty. Her stomach clenched hard and she caught her balance by holding onto a post.

"Where is my horse?" she asked.

"Ain't got one, *ma'amselle*," he replied. "Mistress sold her at market last week."

Rose jerked as if she had been slapped.

"Said you had no more need of her."

Tears welled in her eyes; bile rose in the back of her mouth. She kept her wits about her and bobbed her head at the stable boy, her knuckles white as she unpeeled her fingers off the post and clutched the basket with both hands.

"Then I will take the dray mare," she announced.

"No one touches her but me and your lady," he

said, shaking his head. "If *madame* gives you her leave, you can do as you like."

"Very well," she replied. "I—I shall go ask her."

Keeping to the shadows, she crept past the *château*. Then she hurried into her garden. In her mind's eye, the lush, wondrous flower grotto rippled like a stained glass window over the brown-and-green vegetable vines and sturdy beanstalks. She could see again the statue of Artemis and the fountain and the silvery stream. Gone, but still cherished.

She fell to her knees before the faceless scarecrow, where the goddess's statue had stood.

"Artemis," she said aloud. "Please, help me now. I believe I am at the door of death itself and I no longer wish to open it. Please, *je vous en prie*. I am yours, and I beg you to save me."

The blank-faced scarecrow stared down at her. Rose's hands trembled hard. Just as she began to panic, a small voice whispered, "*You are loved.*"

She looked down.

Another tiny purple bud had pushed through the surface of the rows of cabbages.

Little brown hooves moved into her field of vision; as she looked up, a small brown doe blinked its enormous eyes at her; then glowed with white light as its eyes turned blue. As Rose watched, it moved toward her. Then it carefully opened its mouth around the little bud, pulled it from the earth, and dropped it at Rose's knees.

Slowly Rose reached down and picked it up. The

deer pawed the earth once, as if impatient to be off.

"All right then," Rose whispered as she cradled the flower in her palm. "Lead me. Tell me where to go."

The doe turned around, then looked back over its shoulder at her as it stepped forward, toward the forest.

"Death waits for me there," Rose protested.

The doe took another step. A breeze whispered, *"If you know true love, you shall not die."*

"As you wish," Rose whispered. She got to her feet, put the rosebud in her pocket, and followed.

EIGHT

In the Land Beyond . . .

The court painter and his wife made haste to prepare their *château* for the return of His Majesty. Fully recovered from the assassination attempt during the hunt, King Jean-Marc wished to reward them for their hospitality, for he had been carried from the forest to their *château* and stayed with them for several days. It was a formal occasion and he arrived with his retinue of groomsmen and guards. His chief advisor, Monsieur Sabot, had arranged the occasion and rode beside the king in his glittering coach.

The painter and his lady bowed deeply as Jean-Marc stepped regally onto their land. Jean-Marc knew *madame*, and his heart hurt a little at the sight of her. Claire had served Lucienne as a lady-in-waiting and married the painter after he came into the king's service. She carried a little bouquet of the most exquisite roses he had ever seen. They were a royal purple, velvet and jewellike.

Upon his approach, she gazed up at him joyfully and cried, "Your Majesty, we bid you welcome. Oh sir, come and see! It is a miracle!"

He looked from Claire to her husband. A tall, blond man, his name was Reginer Marchand, and he was from the Forested Land.

Knitting his brows, Monsieur Sabot stepped forward. "What is this?" he asked Monsieur Marchand.

Monsieur Marchand bowed even lower and said, "With all due respect and deference, Monsieur Sabot, this concerns . . . a situation . . . from a time before I came to court. And so, I must leave the matter to my wife."

Monsieur Sabot frowned. Jean-Marc raised a brow. Then Claire touched the petals of the purple roses and said, "I must prepare you, sire. There is a woman . . . oh, come and see!"

"Perhaps I should go first," Monsieur Sabot said prudently.

But Jean-Marc gave him a wave to signify his indulgence. Bemused, he allowed Claire to escort him through the lovely *château*. He smelled paint and turpentine.

They went into a room Jean-Marc had not seen on his previous visit. A quick glance told him it was Monsieur Marchand's art studio. Canvases and painting supplies lined the walls and drop cloths protected the floor.

"Look," Claire urged Jean-Marc, leading him around to face the canvas.

It was a portrait of a delicate woman with hair of silvery-gold and eyes of starry midnight blue.

She was the exact likeness of Lucienne, dead for more than two years.

"By my father Zeus," Jean-Marc blurted. And then his heart whispered, *Artemis, Artemis, Artemis,* three times in quick succession, in time with his thundering pulse.

He staggered backward and would have fallen, but someone placed a chair behind him. He wasn't certain that he was breathing. He could hear nothing, see nothing but the portrait, and the memory of his lost love. The wound of grief inside him gave him such pain that he gasped aloud. And yet, seeing the face of his beloved stabbed him through the heart with an equal measure of joy.

It *was* Lucienne, down to her eyebrows and her small, straight nose. Down to the curve of her mouth.

He forgot how to breathe. How to think. He was adrift, drowning. He could not see the surface of the river of his life. He didn't want to. He wanted to see only . . . her.

Seeing the king's confusion, Claire said, "Your Majesty, this is a woman who sold some roses to my husband."

The lady was delicate and beautiful and wearing clothes of mourning. She held an armful of purple roses, identical to the ones Claire Marchand still carried.

Then reason rushed into his mind as air rushed into his lungs. He was a fool if he dared to hope so. This was no phantom. This was coincidence and nothing more. "Refashioned by his artist's eye into the very picture of the queen," Jean-Marc said tightly. "To please me."

"*Mais non,*" Claire told the king. Her eyes were shining. "That is the miracle, Your Majesty. If you please, Reginer came into your court *after* the death of my lady. He has never seen her." Jean-Marc himself had ordered all painting and sculptures of Lucienne to be put away, for he could not bear to look at them. No one but the priests and Jean-Marc himself were allowed to see her effigy.

"Even so, sire," Marchand told him. "I have never seen the likeness of Her Late Majesty. My wife informed me that this lady resembles the late queen, may she rest in peace, only after I completed the portrait. I swear that I have painted the woman of the roses exactly as she looks."

Jean-Marc's lips parted. He looked from Marchand to the portrait and back again. He felt more than he had ever felt in his life—love, despair, and more love. It hit him all at once just how much he had missed Lucienne. It was as if, drowned in loss, his grief had muted all his emotions into gray. But he saw now that each one had a color. His grief was deep purple, and his love, a deep shade of pink. Rose-colored. The colors danced and shifted like the pieces of glass inside a kaleidoscope and it was dizzying. He thought he might faint.

He was silent for a long time. He could hear the others waiting for him to continue. He knew they would willingly wait all day and night, if need be. He was the king.

"Who is she?" he asked.

"I know not," Marchand informed him. "I found her in the graveyard in a village."

His scalp prickled as he gazed at the woman. "Graveyard? Is she a ghost then?"

"No ghost, sir. She was tending the roses."

"What village?"

"It's near my father's *château*," he said. His face fell. "I had thought to visit him but I did not go." His forehead knit, and his shoulders drooped. "I lost heart, sir, and then when I met this young woman, I was moved to return at once and paint her."

The king stared at the painting. Monsieur Marchand's dealings with his father were his own affair. But surely this woman was a gift from Artemis herself. Had she not promised him love, if he would only hope?

"Take me to her. Let me see her for myself," the king ordered.

Monsieur Sabot cleared his throat. As the king glanced at him, his advisor reluctantly shook his head.

"With all due respect, my liege, you know that I, among all your advisors, have pressed you to entertain matters of the heart. Every part of my soul rejoices in this miraculous appearance, for I, of course, knew the queen, may she rest in the arms of the gods, and I concur that this beauty is her twin. Nothing would please me more than that you should meet her." Monsieur Sabot hesitated.

"And yet?" Jean-Marc said.

"The mobs continue to gather at our gates. And you heard the reports of your spies. The Pretender has finished training his soldiers. He'll march any day. You must remain in the castle and prepare for an attack." He took a deep breath. "This may be a trick to lure you out."

Monsieur Marchand caught his breath. "Surely, *monsieur*, you do not accuse me of playing traitor to my liege lord."

"Indeed not," Monsieur Sabot assured him. "It is just . . . perhaps a lady who resembles Her Majesty was put in your way."

"So that he would paint her?" Claire Marchand asked. "That makes no sense. Who could guarantee that my husband would be moved to do so? Besides, he never knew Her Majesty."

"Perhaps I could search for her myself," Monsieur Marchand suggested. "I used to live near that village."

"*Hélas*," Claire Marchand murmured. "I fear for you, my husband, if war is coming."

Monsieur Sabot bowed over his leg and said, "Send me, milord. I knew your lady. Once I find this woman, I can bring her to the palace, if indeed she resembles Her Majesty so closely."

Jean-Marc stared at the portrait. "Go at once," he said.

Moving farther and farther away from Ombrine and the *château*, Rose followed the white doe into the forest that held such terror for her, now that she was convinced her stepmother meant to kill her. The trees swallowed up the sunlight, and the doe's soft glow showed Rose the way among the thick roots and brambles. Thunder rumbled. They continued on. Thunder rumbled again.

And strangely, the ground shook.

The doe looked at her. The ground shook again and again; the thunder was so loud it buffeted her ears.

Then she realized that it was not thunder she was hearing. It was the sound of drums.

Her blood froze.

"Soldiers," she whispered.

The doe lowered its head as if to say, *Even so.*

On the slope below, footfalls pounded. A hundred. Two hundred. The trees shifted and weak sunlight filtered in. Endless rows of armed men in dark green shirts, metal breastplates, and helmets marched past. One soldier held a white pennant. It was emblazoned with an elaborate dark green P.

The Pretender!

The white doe turned brown again. A massive brown buck dashed from the forest and trotted up beside her. Another joined her. Then another. Soon half a dozen stalwart deer emerged from the shadows, keening beneath their breaths as they formed a protective circle around her. The doe gently butted her side, and all the deer began to walk up the slope. Rose climbed with them; then, when they reached level ground, the deer broke into a trot. Barefoot, Rose tried to keep up. They crashed through the undergrowth, flattening it for her. They bent back tree limbs so she could pass unharmed. The little doe bleated at her— *whee, whee*—as if urging her to hurry.

They burst out of the forest, past Rose's garden. Ahead, the outline of the *château* rose against a storm-tossed sky. The roof was ablaze. Flames licked the clouds and smoke boiled from the upper-story windows.

"*Au secours!*" Rose screamed.

The deer pressed her onward. Surrounded by a dozen soldiers on horseback, a glittering coach sat below the stony terraces. Six ebony horses with braided manes clacked their hooves on the pitted stones as they whinnied and reared. The coachman, straining to control them, did a double take when he saw Rose and the deer, and shot up straight to his feet.

"Monsieur Sabot!" he shouted. He gestured to Rose. "*Mademoiselle!* To me! Come to me!"

On the terrace above, the front door to the burning *château* burst open. Ombrine and Desirée emerged, laden down with hats and cloaks. Each staggered beneath an oversized bundle, coughing and waving smoke from her path.

A tall, gray-headed man carrying a large black velvet hat and an ornate walking stick came after them. As he caught sight of Rose, he froze. He gaped at her, then gestured with his stick at the coach.

"By Father Zeus!" he bellowed. "*Alors!* To the coach, *mademoiselle!*"

The herd of deer wheeled off, hooves clattering on the gravel. Two of the riders galloped over to Rose and dismounted.

"*Pardon, je vous en prie,*" the taller of the two said to Rose. He took Rose's little basket in his gauntleted hand and passed it to his fellow. Then he gazed down at her feet, which were cut and bleeding, and lifted her up in her arms. He smelled of sweat and leather, and his breastplate was cold. Uncertainly, she put her arm around his neck; his heavy metal boots crunching the gravel as he carried her to the coach.

The waiting footman yanked open the coach door, his face pale. "If you please, *mademoiselle*, quickly," he said.

Rose's escort climbed up the two steps and deposited her carefully against the padded leather seat. Her elbow brushed a wooden chest placed between her and a window covered with black-and-gold velvet.

"*Mademoiselle,*" the man added, passing her basket to her. Bewildered, she settled it in her lap.

To her great alarm, Ombrine and Desirée tumbled in soon after with their large bundles. They reeked of smoke. The old man followed. Once all were inside, one of the soldiers slammed the door shut. After an instant, the coach took off as Rose lifted the velvet curtain. The *château* was blazing. She was cut to the quick and hot tears spilled down her cheeks.

"I am so sorry," the old man said. "It was put to the torch to prevent the Pretender from taking it. Such is war."

"Ah," Rose said, weeping. Memories washed over her. She thought of her mother and Elise and, far more dimly, her father. And of the story of Ombrine and Desirée Severine. This was the second house they would lose to fire. Surely that would make them harder and meaner. But as for Rose herself, her grief softened her, and as she smelled the death of her house in the smoke, she wondered about the little creatures who must have lived in its walls and foraged in it gardens.

Adieu, she bade the house, the gardens, as the coach pulled away and the image receded. *Farewell, all.*

"I am sorry," the man said again. She had no idea who he was and assumed he was a neighbor, come to save the Marchand women.

The wheels clattered on the uneven stones, jostling Rose and her fellow passengers. Desirée was staring at Rose in shock, as if she had never seen her before. Shadows darkened Ombrine's face. But her spine was ramrod straight and her knuckles were white.

The old man turned to Rose. His eyes widened in his wrinkled face, and tears welled. Rose drew back slightly, grateful for the shield of her basket.

"It *is* you," he said, sweeping off his hat with a courtier's grace. "Zeus is mighty indeed."

"*Comment?*" Rose asked. She gripped her basket tightly. "Please, sir, what do you mean?"

A huge booming sound rocked the coach. Desirée screamed and grabbed onto Ombrine.

"They're attacking us!" she shouted.

"*Oui*," the man replied grimly.

Battle cries and more explosions pummeled the coach, followed by a steady *thunk-thunk-thunk*.

"Are those arrows?" Ombrine asked. Her voice was almost calm.

The man's silence was his assent. "We have a loyal armed escort and our coachman is very skilled," he said.

"What of the footman?" Rose asked.

"The soldiers will shield him."

"My daughters are my life." Ombrine pulled Desirée close as she reached forward for Rose's hand. Rose stayed as she was, her fingers around her basket handle. "If harm should come to either one of them . . ."

"What if they capture us?" Desirée cried. "And . . . and have their way with us?" Her eyes gleamed.

"Desirée, *please*," Ombrine said in a falsely demure singsong tone. "There is a gentleman present."

"But what if they *do*?"

"They shall not," the man replied. "Surely the gods watch over us." He turned to Rose, his eyes searching her face. A single tear slid down his cheek. "This is beyond the ability of one to fathom. She is the very like."

Rose licked her lips and glanced at Ombrine, wondering if this was something of her devising. If this man was to be her accomplice, unwitting or not, in some kind of trap.

"This is my stepdaughter, as I have explained," Ombrine cut in. "Rose, *ma chérie*, it seems that you sold some of your exquisite purple roses to the royal court painter. He was so taken by your loveliness that he painted your portrait. And now the king wishes to meet you."

Rose gaped at her. Heat washed over her cheeks. "I did meet a man," she began. "In the village graveyard."

"You sold him some purple roses," Ombrine continued.

"For nearly a hundred *sous!*" Desirée put in. Then she grimaced as her mother shot daggers at her. "Or so I recall your telling us."

"Indeed, I never did tell you," Rose said boldly. She would not heap a lie upon her lie, not at this point in their game. Ignoring Desirée, she turned to the man. "I pray you, sir, explain to me what is happening."

"Rose, *ma petite*," Ombrine said. "Show respect. This man is . . . significant."

"You . . . are not His Majesty the king?" Rose asked.

He shook his head. "I am Edouard Sabot, chief advisor to His Majesty. And it is as I told your stepmother." He couldn't take his eyes off Rose. "One may have heard that Her Majesty, the late queen, died of childbed fever some years ago."

The coach bounced and rocked. Horses whinnied. *Thunk-thunk-thunk.* Men shouted. One screamed in pain. Or terror.

"*Monsieur.*" Rose balanced herself by grabbing onto the box. "Please, I beg of you, continue."

"What's in there?" Desirée demanded, pointing at the box. "Jewels?"

"Weapons?" Ombrine asked.

The man gazed at the box. "The late queen passed away, taking her little son with her, and the king fell into deep grief. His enemies have made much of his single state—and his lack of heirs—and I, among many others, have begged him to remarry. But his heart would not permit it."

"Until he saw your portrait," Ombrine said in the same falsely pleasant tone. "And now he is besotted with you, Stepdaughter."

Rose's lips parted. Her brows went up as the man nodded.

"You are the living embodiment of Her Majesty Queen Lucienne," he told her gently. "You could be her twin." His gaze traveled over her face, her hair, her hands gripping her basket. "Indeed, you could be Lucienne herself."

"And that is why . . . His Majesty . . . sent for me?" She trailed off, utterly astonished.

He said, "In that box, there is a gown for your first meeting with the king. Lucienne's own seamstress sewed it overnight with her servants, with many, many prayers that the gods were giving you to the king. I brought it with the hope that I would find you and I have."

He smiled. "Father Zeus is merciful. When we arrive at the palace, you may change into it then." He cleared his throat. "There is more I wish to tell you. About your family. As I mentioned, the woman who created the gown was seamstress to the queen. And her husband is your—"

But at that moment, a huge cry rose up around the coach. It wobbled and shook and the right side dipped as the left side rose up off the ground. Desirée screamed as her mother slammed against her and the two crashed against the wall. Monsieur Sabot slid into Rose, pushing against the box. Her head smacked wood; she saw a bright light, and then all went black.

Rose woke to velvet on her cheek. And to screaming. And to a whisper.

"*Vite, vite.*"

Rose opened her eyes to find a brown doe gazing down at her. She bolted upright. Monsieur Sabot, Desirée, and Ombrine lay unconscious in a tangle beside her.

"*Alors*, Monsieur Sabot." She reached for the elderly man. "Sir, wake up. We must get out of here!"

"*Non.* Leave him," something whispered against her ear, as the deer nudged her again.

The coach had fallen into a rut mere feet away from a wooden bridge spanning a rushing river. The coachman, the footman, and several of the guards were attempting to right it. A few yards away, the remainder of the king's men clashed on horseback with the first line of the Pretender's foot soldiers. Crimson blood splashed a black-and-gold breastplate as an arrow caught one of the soldiers in the chest and he tumbled from his horse.

"*Vite,*" came the whisper again, and the deer stared

hard at Rose. Slowly, woozily, Rose got to her feet.

Lightning flashed overhead, and rain began pouring down on battling men, the deer, and Rose like a waterfall. The deluge was so strong and unexpected that Rose nearly lost her balance. She grabbed on to the little doe's back as she shielded her head.

Then, to her utter amazement, the deer gathered up the hem of her skirt. It turned and began trotting across the road. Stumbling behind reluctantly, Rose gazed over her shoulder at Monsieur Sabot, Ombrine, and Desirée.

"They have a god," the voice whispered through the rising wind and rain. *"The god of the Severines will protect them."*

But it was clear to Rose that the battle was hopeless. The Pretender's men outnumbered the king's a hundred to one. What would they do to the king's loyal advisor and two defenseless women?

"They are not defenseless. Wait and see."

She tried to go back but the deer held her fast as it picked up speed. Then it made a wheezing sound and raced down the embankment toward the river.

Hoofbeats pounded behind Rose. The deer dragged her closer to the rushing water.

Rose glanced over her shoulder. On the horizon, the clouds moved and boiled. But they were not clouds. They were large blackbirds. Hundreds of them. They were falling from the sky like stones, swooping down on the Pretender's men with sharp claws extended and beaks aimed at the men's eyes. Rose cried out and covered her eyes with her hand, and the deer yanked harder.

"*Et voilà,*" said the voice. "*Now have no fear. Remember that a wish was made. A lesson must be learned. And then all will be well.*"

Hoofbeats shook the ground. Hot breath steamed against the back of her neck; she looked over her shoulder to see a mounted knight in the Pretender's colors. His sword was raised over his head as he galloped straight at her.

The deer tugged insistently and Rose lost her footing. Down she tumbled onto her side, rolling in the rain, sliding in the mud. Then before she realized what was happening, she fell into the river.

The icy water shocked the breath out of her. Her sodden skirts dragged her down, down, and she went under, tumbling end over end, having no idea where the surface was, where the river bottom. She gasped, gulping in water, flailing as the river threw her at churning rocks and tree stumps wide as coach wheels. Within an instant, she was battered senseless and out of air, and her helpless body quit the fight. Limp and dazed, she hurtled along as her eyes closed again.

I am going to die, she thought.

"*If you believe in true love, you shall not die,*" the voice relied.

And then, something glowed beneath her eyelids.

NINE

In the Land Beyond . . .

"Attack!" cried the soldier on the wall, just before the arrow slammed into his chest. He fell backward with a shout as blood blossomed across his chain mail like a rose.

From a position high above in the barbican, King Jean-Marc drew his battle sword from its scabbard. In full battle armor, he lunged for the door, but his bodyguard stretched out his gauntleted hand to bar the way. Lightning crackled, revealing grim purpose in the man's expression.

"Milord, I pray you, stay here."

"I am a warrior," Jean-Marc said, flipping the visor of his plumed helmet over his face, "and I will not turn my back on the battlefield."

"Be that as it may, sir," the bodyguard replied as lightning cracked and crackled again, "but with all due reverence and respect, you are the only king we have. And we are fighting the Pretender to keep you on the throne. If you die, our cause is lost, whether six or six hundred of us survive the battle."

A thunderous explosion pummeled the barbican,

throwing the bodyguard against the king. Then the door blasted inward and Jean-Marc instinctively threw the man out of the way. A piece of wood as long and sharp as a spear pierced Jean-Marc's shoulder where metal met leather; blood gushed like a silvery stream and he grunted as he pulled it out.

"The royal coach!" someone shouted. "It's coming!"

Jean-Marc staggered into the ruined doorway and shielded his eyes, scanning the storm-tossed horizon. An arrow shot past his cheek. The rain pummeled his armor like fists.

Once he reached the parapet, he gazed down on the scene. The forest was on fire, and the rolling hills beyond the castle boiled with smoke and steam. The distant shape of a coach and six horses bobbled through the hazy downpour. At least a dozen men on horseback chased after it.

But what was this? An enormous flock of black-birds broke from the rain clouds. There had to be hundreds, with wingspans as broad as Jean-Marc's shield. They fell upon the attackers and their horses, harrying and distracting them.

A miracle sent from the gods, surely.

"*Allons-y*," Jean-Marc told the bodyguard.

"Your Majesty, it is better that you remain here," the man said diffidently.

Jean-Marc gestured at the coach and its retinue of blackbirds. "I shall not," he insisted. If the gods were truly kind, Monsieur Sabot sat in that coach, with the lady of the roses.

"You are my king," the bodyguard said. "I am yours to command."

King and bodyguard flew down the stairs in concert. The courtyard raged with chaos; in the sheets of rain, Jean-Marc's bowmen, in black and gold, let fly a barrage of flaming arrows at a throng of enemy soldiers in dark green. A crowd of green-shirts heaved a battering ram against the portcullis.

"To the horses," he yelled, and his bodyguard nodded.

The king's warhorse, La Morte, awaited him in the stable. The bodyguard took another massive steed and the two rode out to the burning road.

Swords flashing, king and subject mowed the foot soldiers down as if they were straw men, and blasted through the phalanx of archers. In that moment Jean-Marc was certain he was the favored son of Zeus, for it was a miracle that he hadn't been wounded again, and that the gash in his shoulder had not grown worse.

Hélas, his bodyguard was not so favored. An arrow caught him in the chest and he tumbled off his horse. The enemy closed in around him as lightning crackled like the triumphant laughter of the god of death.

Jean-Marc clenched his mouth in a thin line. On any other day, he would have ridden back for his man. But not for his kingdom would he trade the safety of the lady he prayed was in the coach. He rode on, swinging his sword at all comers, and galloped hard through a cluster of the Pretender's knights on horseback. As they wheeled in pursuit, he made for the road.

His heart leaped when he saw the familiar silhouette of Monsieur Sabot on the driver's seat. Birds wheeled above him, but did not attack. Monsieur Sabot saw him, and Jean-Marc galloped in front of the lead horses, indicating to his advisor that he would escort them in.

Perhaps troubadours would sing of the next few moments, for it seemed to the king that he fought like Ares himself. The god of war moved his sword and his horse as he flung the enemy from the path leading into the courtyard. He mowed down untold numbers of enemies, caught countless arrows on his shield.

But he and Ares had help, in the form of the large blackbirds that cawed and shrieked, shooting their talons into the eyes of the enemy, clutching arrows in their claws and riding them like the Furies until they landed in the mud. Jean-Marc had never seen the like and he knew the divine was surely with him . . . and that today the Pretender would die.

At last the coach rattled into the courtyard and the portcullis slammed back down. As miraculously as they had appeared, the birds rose in a tremendous, cawing flock back into the stormy sky and flew away.

A half dozen of Jean-Marc's own soldiers swarmed around the coach, brandishing weapons—swords, bows, battle-axes, maces.

"Stand down!" Jean-Marc yelled, opening his face-plate to reveal his identity. "I am your king!"

Huffing and panting in the rain, they lowered their weapons.

Jean-Marc leaped from his horse. His armor weighed him down like an anchor and his shoulder was on fire as he yanked open the coach door.

There she was.

She stood in the door of the coach, dressed in the gown Sabot had brought for her: clouds of white lace embellished with purple rosettes. Her silver-blond hair tumbled loose over her shoulders. Her starry midnight eyes shone as she gazed at him with startled delight. Then she lowered her gaze and swept a curtsy.

"My lady," he whispered. He bent down and took her delicate, trembling hands, mindful of his gauntlets. As he raised her up, lips met lips; he kissed her and his heart thundered. It was Lucienne he kissed. He was certain of it. The gods had brought her back to life for him.

He felt his tears on his cheeks as waves of emotion rolled over him, through him. He felt as if he had been thrown back in a churning river of his own passions and he was breathless.

Which god did this to me, for me? He thought in that moment not of Artemis, but of Eros. Willing lovers bared their breasts for his arrow, heedless of the risk that love would tear their hearts down the middle. *Make her live forever,* he begged no god and all gods. *Make her never leave me again.*

Her fingers worked against his chain mail. Then, catching her breath, she pulled away gently, her face flushed, her eyes downcast. She was crying too. She sank to her knees and buried her face in her hands.

"*Mais, mon amour, qu'est-ce que tu fais?*" he asked, bending low to her.

"Your Majesty," she said, still not daring to look up at him. "Please, sir, my stepsister is missing."

From inside the coach, a dark-haired woman appeared behind her and put her hand on her shoulder. She was weeping uncontrollably.

Monsieur Sabot climbed down off the driver's seat. His face was bruised; blood mottled his cheeks. He said, "Your Majesty, I present to you Rose Marchand." He gazed at Jean-Marc in wonder. "The half sister of the court painter."

"Even so?" Jean-Marc asked, astonished.

"I have a brother?" she asked, gasping.

"My husband's son is here?" the dark-haired woman cried. "Summon him at once, I beg of you! Perhaps he will help us find Desirée."

"This is Ombrine Marchand, stepmother to Rose," Monsieur Sabot continued. "Her daughter is named Desirée. The coach crashed and in the attack, Desirée disappeared. We could not stay and search."

"*Hélas,*" Ombrine whispered. "Oh, my good lord, please help us!"

Jean-Marc nodded. "I will. First we'll take you both to the temple," he said, nodding at Monsieur

Sabot, indicating that he should accompany them. "The priests of Zeus will protect you."

"*Vite*," Monsieur Sabot said, clapping his hands at the king's soldiers. They snapped to, forming a protective square around the king, the two ladies, and Sabot himself. Their heavy metal shoes clanked as they marched through the chaos. The hand of Mademoiselle Marchand rested lightly on Jean-Marc's as he scanned the sky for the large blackbirds.

"Those birds," he said to her. "What of them?"

"Aid from the gods? I pray they watch after my dear stepsister," she replied. Her voice broke and he laid his other hand over hers. But the metal and leather acted as a barrier. His mind raced ahead to the bedroom, and no coverings at all. . . .

Smoke rose from the temple dome as they hurried inside. Three priests in golden togas stood at the altar, which was piled with coins and sacrifices to Zeus: turtledoves and pigeons. Jean-Marc had banished the previous priests, who had foretold a long life and a son for Lucienne. They had been either poor priests or liars and he had no use for either.

"Your Majesty," the chief priest said as the three holy men bowed. "We are honored."

An explosion shook the rafters. Debris and dust sprinkled down. The man glanced at his two fellow priests as they coughed and fanned the air in front of them, trying to keep the altar clear of contamination. "How goes the battle, sir?" he asked.

"We shall prevail," the king replied.

"*Bien sûr*," the priest replied. "Of course. I have cast the runes and victory is foretold."

"That is well," Monsieur Sabot said, stepping in. He gestured to the women. "His Majesty commends to you Madame Marchand and her stepdaughter, Mademoiselle Rose Marchand. They require safe harbor."

"We are at your command, Your Majesty," the priest said to Jean-Marc. "We'll provide food and rooms here in the temple."

"*Merci*," the king said. Though he was loathe to go, he had a battle to win and a stepsister to rescue. "Sabot, you're with me."

Monsieur Sabot bowed. "As you wish, Your Majesty."

Jean-Marc regarded the lovely woman, tearstained and distraught. Then a breeze whispered against his ear, "*Marry her.*"

Startled, he frowned at the chief priest and said, "Did you speak?"

"*Non*, Your Majesty," the man replied with a bow. He looked a trifle confused. "I only said that we are yours to command."

"*Marry her. Immediately.*"

The king blinked. He looked left and right. Then up at the statue of Zeus, his god. Zeus's features remained impassive. Serene and wise. And yet ... had the lips moved? Was the god directing this? Artemis had promised him that he would love again. And then, in the most amazing of coincidences, Reginer Marchand's own half sister was the twin of Lucienne, and she and her brother had met without realizing who each other was. Surely, the divine was at work. Surely, he should listen and obey.

And yet it was so sudden and so strange . . . he wondered at such haste.

"It is the next step in my Best Beloved's journey," the voice insisted. *"You must play your part."*

And who could say if the breeze spoke of Desirée or the missing daughter of Laurent and Celestine? Who could know if it was the messenger of Artemis who urged Jean-Marc to marry the imposter? Or was it an ally of the shadows who spoke for Desirée?

Could it possibly have been both? Do journeys sometimes weave between the darkness and the light?

Listening in either case, Jean-Marc turned to her and said, "Madame, you know me not at all. But I feel that I know you. And I have just heard my god's voice telling me that we are to marry at once."

The three priests caught their breath. It was not in the nature of Father Zeus to speak directly to anyone save those who had dedicated their lives to his service. It was unheard of that He would speak to anyone else, not even a king.

"Sire, we're in battle," the chief priest protested hesitantly. "A wedding at such a time would be unseemly."

"It must be now," Jean-Marc insisted. "Unless the Rose Bride objects."

Despite her anguish, the lady's face glowed with

light, like the luminous spirit he had met in the forest.

With a tremulous smile, she cupped her unsteady hand against his cheek. "I must confess Your Majesty, that when you kissed me, I felt in my heart that we are married already or that we had been before." Her voice caught. "I know not how. It makes no sense. . . ."

His chest swelled. His eyes teared. He cupped her hand with his own.

"But Your Majesty, you have been in battle and you are tainted with death," the priest objected.

"Then purify me. You are my priest, but I am your king."

"Do as he says," Monsieur Sabot interjected. He gazed at the pair, pleased and astonished, and over at the stepmother, whose face betrayed a hundred emotions—joy for her stepdaughter, terror for Desirée.

The priests slid disapproving glances at each other. Then the chief priest said, "As you wish, sire. You are our liege."

Jean-Marc was taken away. His shoulder was stitched up and he was given a ritual bath, perfumed, and dressed in the only fresh clothing they had, which was a white toga bordered in gold. They wrapped his feet in leather sandals. The two lesser priests lit candles and incense, and chanted the same hymn that the boys' choir had sung for Lucienne, bidding her come to her bridegroom.

As the moon beamed down and the sounds of dying men and horses rattled the temple, the rite was performed according to the older ways. The pair's hands were bound together, their wrists slashed so that their blood mingled into a large golden cup.

Jean-Marc gazed at the Rose Bride as she clenched her teeth and made her hand into a fist so that she would bleed harder, whispering, "I want my blood in your veins. I want to carry your son."

For a moment, he was thrown back to the moment of his wife's death, and along with her, the death of his son. He thought, *What am I doing? What have I done?*

Then the moment passed and Jean-Marc clenched her bloody fingers with his own. He said, "If the god wills it, your son will be a king."

"Your Majesty, I beg of you," the chief priest murmured, "speak no more for the god. Such is not our way."

Jean-Marc bit off his sharp retort. He knew the priest was right. It was simply that he was filled with such deep wonderment and love that he felt almost as if he had been bewitched.

"You are one," the chief priest announced.

The woman sank into Jean-Marc's arms and kissed him full on the lips. His heart sang. Then he felt a deep pain in the center of his heart, perhaps the thorn that came from loving the Rose Bride. He told his soul that this was a miraculous moment, as the gods returned his true love to him. But grief had been his companion for so long that it clung to him, afraid to leave.

"I must to the battle now," he told her. He turned to Monsieur Sabot. "Call for my squire to fetch my armor." He turned to his bride. "Give me a purple rose from your dress for a favor," he said.

She burst into fresh tears as she tore a rosette from the gown. As she held it out to him, her legs gave way and she would have fallen, if her stepmother hadn't grabbed her arm.

"Do not die," she begged him. "Do not."

"It will be as the gods will," the chief priest said quickly.

"As you say," Jean-Marc replied.

As the king strode in full armor into the castle courtyard, the sky lit up with fire and moonlight. The purple rosette on his breastplate looked black. His peacocks and monkeys shrieked in concert with the screams of wounded and dying men. A soldier with a jagged cut across his face bobbed a bow as he ran past the king, and Jean-Marc unceremoniously grabbed his arm.

"How do we fare?" he asked.

The man's cheeks were coated with blood and grime. The cut was deep, and would leave a large scar. He swallowed hard and shook his head.

"Not well, Your Majesty."

"The tide will turn now," Jean-Marc promised the

man. "Go and tell the others that the king says so."

The exhausted man's eyes glimmered with hope. Jean-Marc gave him an encouraging nod. The man started to nod back, but his hope had not become as strong as faith. He bowed and ran back toward the courtyard.

Jean-Marc turned his head in the direction of the royal burial vault, thinking of Lucienne and their child in her coffin and of her twin in the temple of Zeus.

Hoofbeats thundered toward him. His warhorse, La Morte, galloped toward him, danced sideways, and chuffed at his master. He was still saddled.

Jean-Marc put his foot in the stirrup and hoisted himself onto the massive stallion's back. He took up the reins and clicked his teeth. The horse reared high, his front hooves kissing the hem of the moon as it hung in the sky.

He raced past the domes and spires of the castle, beyond the cultivated gardens, along the rectangular reflecting pool to the clearing, where the trio of stone deer grazed at the sopping grass. Behind them, the marble statue of Artemis, protectoress of women, stood with her arrow notched against her bow. Lucienne herself had erected the statue when he had brought the devotion of Artemis to the ladies in the court.

"My lady," Jean-Marc said. He trembled as he dismounted. "I heard your message and I obeyed. I fear that my own god will punish me for attending to you.

Therefore, I put my trust in you, Artemis, patron of women. My queen died and yet she lives. Protect her now. Let me kill my enemy."

The pipes and drums of the Pretender drew near. The ground shook. Jean-Marc got to his feet and turned around.

There, on the rise beyond the trees, the vast hordes of the Pretender's army raced for the castle. There were thousands of them, perhaps tens of thousands. The king's soldiers poured out of the castle yard, meeting the Pretender on the field. The enemy moved like snakes, sure and bold; they marched like men who loved their leader and knew their cause was just.

Clouds broke apart and the heavy full moon shone down on the battlefield. Jean-Marc held his breath, waiting for the flocks of blackbirds. But they did not come. Instead, a falling star arched across the sky. Then another and another: Artemis' arrows, shot from heaven by the goddess's own hand.

The stars sparkled against the helmet of a single armored warrior on a pure white horse. It held a lance pointed straight up to the heavens. Moonlight surrounded it in a white-blue circle.

For a moment, Jean-Marc thought the warrior was the luminous being he had seen in the forest. Then a pennant attached to the lance flapped in the night breeze. It was emblazoned with a P.

The Pretender himself.

He whistled for La Morte. The horse cantered

over to him. Jean-Marc climbed back on, put his heels to the stallion's flanks, and rode forward to head up his army. He pushed La Morte to a full gallop. He heard the men screaming their battle cries; the drums pulsing, the pipes shrieking.

Moonlight bathed him as he broke from the trees. His attention was fixed on the Pretender. His enemy lowered his lance and pointed it directly at Jean-Marc. Heads turned—a hundred, a thousand.

"Vive le Roi Jean-Marc!" the army bellowed. *"Jean-Marc là bas!"* the other side shouted.

The Pretender rode straight for him. Arrows flew from Jean-Marc's archers, and missed. Then his foot soldiers jabbed at the Pretender's horse with spears and pikes, and missed.

The knights came at him with swords, maces, and lances . . . and missed.

The Pretender barreled through the lines as if they were phantoms unable to touch him.

He made for Jean-Marc. The king stood his ground.

Then the moon shifted and the two adversaries glowed like gods. The Pretender shimmered like one of Artemis's celestial messengers, and Jean-Marc did, as well.

Awestruck, the drummers left off first, followed by the pipers. As the fighters saw their two leaders transformed by light, their battle broke off. One of the king's men, brandishing an ax, stepped away from his fallen foe and allowed him to get to his feet.

Across the muddy field of battle, weapons clanked as they were lowered. Horses whinnied and pawed the ground, confused and eager to get back into the fray.

King and usurper faced each other alone on the field of honor.

No one spoke. No one moved.

As the two regarded each other, an arrow whizzed past Jean-Marc's ear and slammed into the neck piece of the Pretender's helmet. The force shattered it. Blood spurted from his neck like a fountain.

The Pretender dropped from his horse with a crash.

A collective gasp of dismay rose from the Pretender's men.

No one moved on the entire field of battle as shock rippled through the attack forces. This was the Pretender's cause, his battle. Now he would never be king.

Jean-Marc galloped to the fallen knight. La Morte's mighty hoofbeats were the heartbeats of every man who watched. Aware of the excruciating tension, which could revert to chaos at any moment, the king dismounted. Goose bumps rippled over his flesh as he knelt over the Pretender and took off his helmet.

Jean-Marc had heard the rumor that the Pretender looked exactly like his father, Henri III. But the man didn't look a thing like Jean-Marc's father or his first queen, Isabelle. His eyes were blue, his mouth thin and scarred. He had pockmarks on his cheeks and forehead. Jean-Marc wondered if he'd arranged for someone who more closely resembled his father to show himself to the people in his name.

And the arrow in his neck was the stone arrow of the statue of Artemis.

The Pretender blinked once. His life's blood gushed from the hole like a fountain, and Jean-Marc started to press his fingertips against it to staunch the flow.

The Pretender's blue eyes turned toward him. Jean-Marc kept his hand at his side. This man was his enemy. He had challenged the legitimate line of the kings of the Land Beyond. He deserved to die. The goddess herself had decreed it.

And who are you, mortal man, to interpret the words of the gods?

Jean-Marc staunched the flow, his gauntlet warming with the man's blood. He felt the pulse of the Pretender's heart, wondered who he had really been and if he had had a claim.

But it was too late to save him. The man gasped once and then he died.

Jean-Marc stood.

His warriors cheered and raised their spears, clashed their swords against their shields. Wave upon wave of sound undulated across the battlefield. Horses reared and whinnied; knights pranced them in circles.

The Pretender's men broke into a rage. Faces contorted with fury and anger, they charged the king's own. Cheated by a woman's god! They owed Artemis no loyalty, no love! And her favorite would not have any.

The two sides roared together, clashed, engaged. A phalanx of knights surrounded Jean-Marc in a protective circle as he hoisted his vanquished enemy from the ground and carried him toward his horse. Two of the knights dismounted and helped him, draping the Pretender's body facedown over La Morte's saddle. Jean-Marc mounted La Morte and took the reins of the other horse, leading him toward the castle courtyard.

He was a warrior, but this night he would turn his back on the battlefield. The Pretender's cause was lost. Perhaps it was the fate of his followers to lose their lives in battle, which was why they resumed their fight. The Pretender's men would fight in vain and die in vain. Jean-Marc knew that his men would carry the day. The goddess had spoken.

And now, to his bride and her family. To rescue her sister and feast the events of this night.

To become a husband again. And if the gods willed, a father.

He shook. The battle inside his heart was the true one, he realized. And it had just resumed.

TEN

Jean-Marc ordered the river to be dredged for his wife's stepsister. Search parties traced the coach's route from the castle to the *château*. Then he purified himself in the baths, receiving absolution from the priests of Zeus for the death of his enemy. Perfumed and oiled, he dressed in his robes of state and stole away to the mausoleum, where the effigy of Lucienne rested on her sarcophagus.

She doth teach the torches to burn bright.

The king knelt and wrapped his hands around her cold marble fingers. He traced the stone rose between her palms. He didn't understand the ways of her goddess. He had no idea what part he was to play in the journey of her Beloved or even if that was what he'd heard. It was unthinkable to him that his journey was not paramount—he was the king. Perhaps he himself was the Beloved of whom the voice had spoken. But he supposed that was what priests were for—to explain the ways of divine if they could. Jean-Marc was not a holy man. He was a warrior king.

Now he made as if to brush the tendrils of hair from her forehead, his rough fingertips sliding over smooth stone. If he closed his eyes, he could hear the steady rhythm of her hairbrush as she ran it through the shimmering gold tendrils.

"I dare to love you again, only you," he whispered to her. "It's not another I take. It's you."

Perhaps the flickering torches created a trick of the light. But as Jean-Marc gazed at the beloved face, he was certain that her marble lips smiled.

He leaned forward and kissed them. His heart caught but this time the pain didn't surprise him. He was becoming accustomed to the strange blend of joy and pain that deep emotion conjured.

Then he called for a feast to celebrate the victory. He knew it was required. He fully expected his wife and stepmother-in-law to stay in seclusion until Desirée was located. The priests were hard at prayer for her safe return and why could that not be so? Miracles were plentiful this day.

His courtiers rushed to make ready for the celebration, thrown into a mild panic as wives and servants pulled doublets and jerkins over bandages and slings. More than one lady tried in vain to chase the stench of smoke from her fine garments. Mud slopped everywhere and the kitchen staff slipped and slid as they slaughtered lambs and calves for the wedding feast.

Despite all the trouble, the castle blazed with joy. The Pretender was dead and the king was married.

Rose jerked awake when she heard the shouting. In the gray haze of daybreak, she lay sprawled on a grassy embankment inches from the churning headwaters of the river. Dizzy, she lifted her head and saw a flotilla of rowboats on the churning river—at least a dozen, all painted a checkerboard design of black and gold. In each boat, a man in livery sat at the oars while two or three other men threw out weighted nets. A cannon boomed from an unseen location around the bend and it made her jump.

She scrambled to her feet. Something was in her mouth. She reached up a hand to inspect it—

—and realized that she had no hands.

With a gasp, she bent her head and stared at her body.

She had legs instead of arms—four long, slender animal legs. Hooves instead of feet and hands. She had been transformed into an animal and her entire body was covered with velvety brown fur.

Rose opened her mouth and let the object inside it drop to the sandy earth. It was the purple rosebud.

"You are loved," it whispered.

She raced to the river's edge and looked down at her reflection. She was so astonished that she darted backward on her long, delicate legs. Then she came back and stared. She was a small brown doe.

She shook from head to hoof. Her heart pounded in her ears. *Am I Rose Marchand no longer?* Had she died and become a messenger of the goddess?

She lifted a hoof and inspected it. The pads on the bottom released a musky scent. Smells whirled around her like leaves in the wind: wood moss, mushrooms, decaying plants, a badger, a spiderweb.

And the men.

Her hearing was as magnified as her sense of smell: One man was muttering about how unfair it was that he should have to dredge the river Vue while other servants feasted. A second fretted that his wife's handsome cousin had taken her to the feast in his place.

Overwhelmed, Rose pranced in place, her tiny, sharp hooves stamping the ground. She heard herself bleating *whew-whew-whew*, the distress call to other deer.

And other deer broke through the underbrush—first a magnificent buck with a huge rack of antlers, then another, lesser buck, then three does. They raced to her and nosed her with their velvet muzzles. They surrounded her and made comforting ticking sounds.

On the ground, the little rose whispered, *"You are loved."*

Artemis, I thank you, she thought. She still thought in French. She was still Rose. Was it so with all the other deer? She tried to speak, but her words came out in deer sounds that meant *I am afraid. I need the herd.*

So she thought the words, *Are you human as well?*

The deer stared back at her without responding.

"Here's something!" one of the men bellowed. "Heavy enough for a body!"

The deer turned and watched as he nodded to his

partner and together they pulled in their net. The rower bent backward to see what they had found.

A thick tree stump strained the dripping, diamond-patterned net. The oarsman laughed while the other men uttered curses in low-class, guttural French and threw the trunk back into the river with a splash.

They are searching for me, she realized. *Did the others make it to the castle?*

The deer gazed at her. Then they turned and began to walk into the forest. Carefully scooping the rosebud back into her mouth, she followed. Forest smells assailed her nostrils—mud and earth and dozens of tiny animals. Wolves had been through there and wild boar. And men. Hunters.

The forest darkened as the herd cantered into an old-growth stand of beeches and oaks. She raced through shadows so thick with animal smells they slid across her fur like hands. The others bleated at her and she ran with them until they blazed through a copse of trees back into golden sunlight. Her nostrils filled with the beloved scent of roses. The smell was as thick as a carpet. It drew her forward and she poked her head through a lacy patchwork of ferns.

About twenty feet in front of her, a lovely stone *château* perched on a hillock. It was covered with trailing roses. Daffodils sprouted along a walkway. The air was layered with perfume.

Charmed, she walked closer. The other deer accompanied her. The gate was open and she nosed her way through it. On the other side, the wall of the *château* revealed a rectangular leaded window. She walked toward it, trying to see inside.

Her own human face gazed back at her. For an instant, she thought it was her reflection, revealing to her that she had been changed back into a woman. But when she tilted her head, the likeness did not.

Then she saw the rest of the portrait—for obviously, that was what it was. She was wearing her black dress. A dozen purple roses filled her arms.

Then she smelled the scent of approaching humans. There were two whose scents she knew well—they stank of sulfur and hatred.

The herd bleated for her to run away into the forest with them. She stood her ground. The lead buck grunted at her in disapproval, a doe nudged her urgently, and then the animals raced off, melting into the darkness.

Figures moved into the room, and Rose's blood ran cold as she watched through the window.

The first was her stepsister, Desirée. She was dressed in a white gown decorated with purple roses and a golden cloak. And Desirée *was* some kind of demon or perhaps a sorceress: For atop her own features, Rose's face seemed to float like a mask. It was spectral, uncanny: There was her own face, worn by the young woman who hated her above all other things. Her starry midnight eyes blinked and beneath them, Desirée's brown eyes blinked as well. She smiled with Rose's lips, yet beneath . . . were those little fangs?

Rose bleated softly and forced herself to silence.

She was terrified. She understood at once that the men in the boats had been dredging the river for *her*. And that Desirée and her mother had woven magic, or sought a god to do it, so that Desirée could masquerade as her. It must be that they thought to replace her, that they had found a means to a third fortune: to install Desirée as the subject of the portrait, for the pleasure of the king.

The second to enter the room was the golden-haired man, who embraced her tenderly, and she laid her head on his chest. What was this? Had he fallen in love with her as well?

Keeping to the shadows, Rose pranced as close as she dared.

". . . Reginer, my dear brother," Desirée said.

Rose blinked rapidly. She had heard that name. She knew her father had a son who had quarreled with him and left. This was he? Was that what Monsieur Sabot had been about to tell her?

That is my half brother. I have family. I am not alone in this world. Artemis, I beg of you, change me back! Let him see Desirée for who she is!

Overcome, she began to pant and paw the earth. She caught herself and forced herself to stop. She was not a real deer. She was a human being.

She bleated in distress, heard herself, clamped her mouth shut. Her tail twitched. Her ears flattened.

"I wished that I had returned years ago," Reginer said sorrowfully. "I would have spared you and your stepfamily from your terrible ordeal."

"But we're here now, together. And the ordeal was not too terrible, Reginer. My stepfamily has loved me so. Oh, if only we can find Desirée safe and sound . . ."

"There, there," he soothed her.

Then Ombrine glided into the room. She was dressed in a magnificent black gown chased with gold. A black veil covered her hair, accentuating her high-boned pallor; she looked more like a mourner than the mother of a bride. Her eyes were puffy with weeping, and she carried a black handkerchief embroidered with red letters: L M.

"We will find her, *madame*," the man said.

"*Merci*," Ombrine murmured. "Oh, children. I would give anything for Laurent to see us all together. I . . . I loved him so. If only Desirée can be found." She fell to weeping.

"There, there, Mother," Desirée sobbed, throwing her arms around Ombrine.

As they embraced, Ombrine turned to face the window. She opened her eyes and Rose saw that they were completely black.

They seemed to stare straight at Rose.

Terrified, Rose bleated softly. She smelled the herd close by. They were waiting for her in the dark forest.

When Ombrine turned her back, Rose darted away and joined them.

The king waited for seven days and seven nights before he began to woo his bride. He understood her grief at the loss of her stepsister. He hadn't called off the search. He would not give up until she was found.

On the eighth day, his lady had sent him a love note and bid him come to her tonight. He had answered that he would.

The king's attendants sprinkled rosewater and apple blossoms on the marriage bed and a virgin placed a corn doll beneath the pillow. Candles were lit and wine was set out.

His bride was in their private apartments with her new ladies-in-waiting, sharing a glass of wine as they brushed her long, golden hair and massaged her shoulders and feet.

Jean-Marc glided through the pleasure garden outside the royal suite. He carried his lute over his shoulder like a young, lovesick swain. The balcony glowed with dozens of candles set in purple paper lanterns. Pomegranate trees sagged with swollen, red fruit. Hummingbirds thronged around the feeder dripping with honey water.

He strummed his lute very softly. Let her think she was hearing things. Let one of her ladies cock her head and listen carefully. One by one, they would realize that the king was in the garden, wooing she who was already won. So it had been with Lucienne. Her ladies had swooned, declaring him the most handsome, romantic prince who have ever lived or loved. They'd teased him and flirted with him, while two of them went to fetch Lucienne, pulling her out to the balcony by her hands, then fluttering away like a covey of doves.

He strummed just a little more loudly. His eyes shone. He was moved beyond himself. His heart was full of sighs and memories. He had come to anticipate the pain and welcome it. For so long, he had felt nothing. Now, sometimes, it was too much. But he welcomed the challenge of deep, strong emotion.

He sang. Of the moon and her eyes; of roses and her lips. He sang of paradise. He missed one note as his mind traveled to the mausoleum and he thought of Lucienne and their babe, lying alone on this night. His joy ebbed *un petit peu*—just a little—and pain rushed in to fill the void.

He panicked *un petit peu*, and missed another note.

Then Desirée walked onto the balcony alone. She didn't bring her ladies to giggle and admire him. She came by herself, graceful as a queen. She wore a long white gown cut low in front, and tucked into her bodice was a dark red rose, very much like the ones he had placed in the hands of Lucienne's effigy, of a dark, heavy night.

He strummed again; she leaned over the balcony and her smile was as luminous as the magical messenger sent to him by the goddess.

"*Je t'aime,*" Desirée said over the sweet sounds of his lute. *I love you.*

"How can you?" he asked in a soft voice as he played. "You don't know me."

She leaned her hand on the balcony. "But I do. I

feel as if I've known you my entire life. I dreamed of you for years. I think the gods were whispering in my ear about the life I was going to have."

Her voice was Lucienne's; her smile, Lucienne's.

"Some say that's what dreams are," he said. "The gods whispering their secrets. Do you worship Artemis?" He held his breath, hoping that her answer would add weight to his belief that she was in some way, his old love.

"Of course," she replied, "but my heart has room for Zeus as well." She smiled sweetly. "And for you."

Joy and grief swirled, deep purple and deep pink. Purple and rose.

His fingers trembled against the strings and he plucked another discordant note. It was like a teardrop in the midst of his happiness.

She held out a hand to him and said, "*Mon amour*, it is late and you must be very tired."

He smiled up at her. The light behind her head made her glow like the favored of Artemis. He strummed his lute gazing at her, reminding himself that this was another woman, a different one; but when he gazed at her, he saw the princess of the Silver Hills. He saw the future he had imagined with her. Her children.

The nightingales sang as he finished his serenade and went back inside the palace to join his bride.

Across the moon large blackbirds flew and cawed, and the candles on the balcony guttered out.

☙ ☙ ☙

Accompanied by her herd, Rose stepped from the shadows and stared up at the darkened balcony. She had been drawn by the music of the lute and the man's deep, wonderful voice.

She knew he was the king. She understood that he had married Desirée because he thought that she was Rose, and that even now they were together in a private garden of love.

What she didn't understand was why she cared. Why it mattered to her that his black hair curled around his ears, his eyes dark and deep-set, his profile strong and familiar. She reasoned that his appearance drew her because she had seen it on the gold coins her own half brother, Reginer, had given her for her roses.

But the coin did him no justice. She had no idea King Jean-Marc of the Land Beyond was so handsome and bore himself so nobly and she was riveted.

Was this love at first sight?

That cannot be, she thought. *Love is a rose that grows over time. It is not a burst of lightning.*

Yet she could not deny that she was thunderstruck.

And that the purple roses had been created in an instant and burst into full boom overnight, many times.

Then she saw a large blackbird fly across the moon and she started. Was magic afoot? The voice had told her that Desirée and Ombrine had their own god and they were not defenseless. Desirée wore a mask—a glamour—and they had convinced the king that she was Rose. Was what she felt for the king—this strong, deep desire—another thread in the spell they had woven?

I want him.

The herd called to her to come away, come away and she turned away from the balcony.

She nickered to the others and followed as they led her to the sleeping place the does had arranged for her. She realized that they knew she was different and they were taking care of her. She was grateful to her soul and she vowed that if one day she had the power, she would forbid all deer to be hunted.

Her tiny purple rosebud had been laid on a bed of rushes, and Rose lay down beside it. The bucks and does gathered around her, one facing her, one facing out, making it clear that they would guard her through the night.

"*You are loved,*" the rosebud whispered.

And as she curled up and drifted off, she thought to herself, *Not by him.*

ELEVEN

In the morning, Rose gazed sleepily down at her hooves, they didn't seem as foreign as they had the day before.

She stirred and lifted her head. Then she blinked her long lashes at the purple rosebush that had grown overnight, from the bud to a fist of three blossoms.

"*You are loved,*" they whispered.

The other deer gathered around her and showed her how to forage for blackberries and mushrooms, and to drink crystal-clear water from a stream.

Refreshed, she bowed her head in thanks to Artemis.

Jean-Marc, she thought. *Jean-Marc of the Land Beyond. That it is his name. He's a man. Men kill deer.*

Those were deer thoughts.

They kill each other.

That was the thought of a young woman who had seen war.

They kill the ones they love.

She didn't know where that came from.

He is not like other men.

Nor that one, and the thought of seeking him out

made her heart beat too fast. She felt woozy and leaned against a mighty oak tree until it slowed down. But it wasn't fear that made her pulse race. It was something else entirely.

He is nothing to me.

And yet, as an image of him filled her mind, she raised her head and sniffed the air in search of his scent.

He is danger.

Her nose found him. The other deer stared at her as if say, *Forget humankind, dear sister. Stay with us.*

Straightening her ears, she trotted among lacy ferns and quivering aspens. The others followed for a time, and then they backed off, wheeling away. Rose gained speed until she was running, and leaped gracefully over a tree stump dotted with lavender and sunflowers. She leaped again, bounding as if her hooves were winged, racing out of the forest with no thought but that he was near.

Danger.

The part of her that had joined the forest—the part of her that thought like a doe—fought against her eagerness. But her human side overruled and she put on a burst of speed as if he was that harbor she sought.

Stop. Turn back! Stop!

As she broke through the last stand of trees and into the daylight, she realized what she was doing and came to a dead stop. She clopped the earth in confusion as she caught her breath. This was madness.

"*Bonjour,* little one," said a voice. "What a surprise."

Jean-Marc stood perhaps twenty feet away, at the

edge of a long pool. He was dressed in a white doublet embroidered with gold over a white tunic and dark blue leggings. In his right hand he held a purple rose. He was smiling like a lighthearted youth.

At her.

If she hadn't been so exhausted, she would have run. But as it was, she could only pant as she caught sight of him. He took a step toward her; she danced backward, but only a couple of faltering steps. She smelled a bit of sulfur mingled with the perfume of the rose and she knew he had been with Desirée. She bobbed her head urgently.

Danger.

"Please, don't be afraid," he said. His voice was very deep and pleasing, like the lower strings of a harp. He held out the rose. "Here. I'm sure this is very tasty."

There was no sulfur on the rose. It was on him. The rose smelled delicious.

She took another step back.

Mild disappointment creased his brow. "*Eh, bien,*" he said, tucking it into his doublet. "I meant it only as a token of thanks to your mistress, queen of the hunt. I assume she lays claim to all deer. Unless, of course, you are her magical emissary. Are you?"

I know not, she thought. *I don't know why I'm here. Why this has happened to me.*

"I have her to thank," he continued, "because she herself has brought my wife back to me."

He looked over his shoulder. Rose chuffed, fearing

that Desirée had accompanied him. But then she saw the spires and domes of the palace in the lavender distance and knew he meant that she was somewhere on the grounds.

"She sleeps," he said, as if Rose had asked aloud. He cocked his head. "Can you understand me? Do you speak French?"

She blinked at him and pawed the ground.

"Does that mean yes?" He bent over his leg with a flourish like a courtier. "If you serve the goddess, please tell her that I am grateful. She told me not to give up hope. *Et voilà.*"

She looked hard at him, urging him to continue. She wanted to know what he had been told.

He ran his fingertips over the rose petals. "We haven't found her stepsister yet. That is the only blot on our joy. Still, the court needs to celebrate." His smile was gentle. "I as well. I've been so long unmarried and now the Rose Bride has bewitched me completely."

Rose bleated. *It* is *witchery,* she thought. *Know me. See me.*

Then she smelled the other deer nearby and fled the king's presence.

Jean-Marc announced seven days and seven nights of celebrations and feasting to mark his marriage and his victory over the Pretender. While he met with Monsieur Sabot and the councillors, his bride busied herself with acquiring a proper wardrobe for her new station in life. Whenever he went to see her, she was draped in fabrics, turning this way on a stool as Reginer's wife, Claire, and her seamstresses took her measurements and made the patterns. She was beaming with delight and he smiled faintly. He couldn't remember Lucienne being as interested in clothes, but she was royal by blood as well as by marriage and was used to the life of nobility.

Gold tissue, rose velvet, yards and yards of lace. Ombrine looked on from a gilt chair upholstered in black, scrolls and papers heaped around her dress and sheaves of pages on her lap.

As Jean-Marc watched quietly from the doorway, Desirée-as-Rose gazed at herself in the mirror, pushing back her blond hair just as he had done the night before.

"Give me that one," Desirée said to Claire, pointing to a bolt of yellow satin. Claire was kneeling beside the lady with a pin in her mouth. She held a piece of vellum and a quill dipped in ink. She was making a dress pattern.

"Yellow? I think not, *madame*," Claire said, shaking her head as one of her assistants picked up the bolt. "It will make you look sallow." She brightened. "I purchased a dress some time ago from a countess. It's such a lovely shade of—"

Desirée stared at her as if she couldn't believe her ears. "Are you disobeying me?"

"Rose," Ombrine remonstrated.

"I want the *yellow*," Desirée insisted. She held out

her hand. "I had a closet full of yellow gowns before the fire. Give it to me. *Now*."

Claire Marchand—who, after all, was the lady's sister by marriage—jerked as if she had been slapped. "I only thought that—"

Desirée turned her gaze from Claire to Jean-Marc, noticing him for the first time. Color blossomed in her cheeks.

"*M'excusez,*" she murmured to Claire. "I'm a little tense. So much has happened." Her lower lip trembled and she bent down, taking the quill from Claire and fidgeting with it.

"She's so worried about her sister," Ombrine said in a half whisper. She turned and saw Jean-Marc. Immediately she leaped to her feet and swept a curtsy. All her lists and papers tumbled off her lap. "Your Highness. I didn't see you there."

Claire and her helpers scrambled to their feet as well, while Desirée curtsied atop the stool. He made a courtly bow in return.

"*Bonjour, mesdames,*" he said. "What is it that you're so busy with?" he politely asked Ombrine.

"I'm taking an inventory of the household, sir." She frowned at his raised eyebrows. "Ought I not? It was the way my husband trained me. I am showing Her Majesty how it's done."

Trembling, she began to gather everything up. Jean-Marc gently stopped her, laying his hands over hers. He was taken aback at how cold she was.

"Please, Mother," he said, offering her the name as

a token of his affection, "it's kind of you to take such an interest." And wholly unnecessary, but he didn't tell her that. He had leagues of secretaries and men of the exchequer to see after his treasury. But he sensed she needed to do something useful to keep her mind off her grief.

"Desirée" had still not been found.

"What do you think, sir?" Desirée asked him. She gestured to the yellow. "Does it make me look sallow?" At her urging, Claire took the bolt and held it beneath Desirée's chin. Both looked to the king for his opinion.

It did make her look sallow. But he said, "If yellow pleases you, you should wear it. You should wear a dozen yellow gowns."

"But does it please *you?*" she asked.

"*Oui.*" He gestured to the other bolts and swaths of fabrics. "What else have you chosen?"

"Many satins, laces, and ribbons, for which I do thank you," Desirée murmured. She hesitated and glanced at Ombrine, who looked uncomfortable.

Jean-Marc gestured for Desirée to speak.

"If you please, we're not sure how to approach this subject with you," she confessed. "But in the matter of my stepsister, we're beginning to lose hope. We're wondering about . . . about . . ." She swallowed back her tears.

Ombrine swept a graceful hand across her own black gown. "It's a delicate situation, sir. Should the queen wear mourning for Desirée?"

He was moved. "Not yet," he said. "We'll keep looking."

"As you wish, Your Majesty." Ombrine swept another curtsy.

"We'll find her," he promised.

"I didn't mean to imply otherwise, Highness." Ombrine touched her fingers to her chest. "Please forgive me."

He wanted to tell his mother-in-law not to be so formal, but that would come in time. He crossed to her and gently raised her from her curtsy.

"After we're finished here, we're going to visit my brother," Desirée told Jean-Marc. Her eyes gleamed. "All at once, I have a brother *and* a husband. It's like . . . magic." She grinned as if at a private joke.

"Like the birds that attacked the Pretender," Jean-Marc agreed. "Surely, the gods favor us."

"Surely," she drawled. She giggled behind her hand.

"Why are you so amused?" Jean-Marc asked her. His brows raised. "Do you have a secret?"

"Of course she doesn't," Ombrine cut in. "A queen tells her husband everything. She is loyal and faithful, and her lord's to command. Is this not so, *Rose?*"

Desirée's smile faded. She cleared her throat and said, "Even so, *Maman.*"

"Your Highness?" It was one of Jean-Marc's councillors, standing diffidently in the doorway. The king's respite was over. It was time to return to affairs of state.

"Ladies, I'll away," he said.

The roomful of women curtsied again.

As he turned, Desirée said in a loud voice, "I think I should skip the yellow. You're quite right, dear sister. It does make me look sallow."

Jean-Marc smiled to himself and left to join the privy council.

Keeping to the trees, Rose found the statue of Artemis at the head of the reflecting pond, where she had met the king that morning. Meeting him had shaken her. She could think of nothing but him. Now that she knew his scent, she smelled it everywhere and when it was free of Desirée's odor, it wove a powerful spell on her. It was intoxicating. It made her daydream of being his bride. Of living in luxury and joy with him, and with her brother.

And with children.

The larks sang like him. The sun glowed like him.

I must find the herd, she thought, seeking comfort. *I must not be alone in this*. She pawed the ground and bleated. No one answered.

Perhaps they had abandoned her because she had dared to approach the king. She didn't know, but she went in search of them. Her nose worked to detect their scents, but Jean-Marc's scent was too overpowering.

As she wandered, she came upon a road. A ramshackle cart pulled by a sway-backed horse stood in the mud. Behind it, a shrieking woman in tatters and rags ran with her arms stretched toward a little boy no more than ten years old. He was sandwiched between two men in livery, and heavy chains weighed down his thin arms.

"It was a loaf of bread!" she shrieked. She stumbled in the mud. "All he took was a loaf! We are starving!"

"It was theft," the taller guard said over his shoulder. "If you worked your fields, you'd have plenty to eat."

"I have no husband to work the fields! Jacques is all I have! We do the best we can!"

The tall guard said nothing, simply yanked on the chain and dragged the boy along. The boy slipped in the mud and fell and the short guard kicked him in the side.

"On your feet!" he bellowed.

"Jacques!" the woman screamed. She ran faster. "Is this the way the king treats his subjects? If it is, better we should have another king! Better that the Pretender had won the day!"

Both guards stopped. They turned. The tall one looked at the short one and a malicious smile broke across his face.

"You know, I've need of a cart and a horse," he said in a low voice to the other man. He dropped the chain and sprinted toward the woman. "You'll be hung for treason for that! And all your goods taken by the Crown!"

"*Maman*, run!" the boy shouted.

Without pausing, the woman threw up her hands.

"Au secours!" she cried. "Help a widow and her orphan!"

Without thinking, Rose broke her cover. She dashed onto the road and charged the tall guard. He tumbled facedown into the mud.

The short guard broke into laughter while the other one sputtered and flailed. Sighting him down, Rose saw murder in his eyes. She read violence in his scent.

Danger! Run!

She nudged the woman, who seemed to understand that Rose meant for her to flee.

"Not without Jacques!' she told Rose. "My boy, save my boy!"

Rose wheeled around and headed for the short guard and the little boy. The guard's eyes grew huge, his mouth dropped open and he sank to his knees in the muck. He let go of Jacques's chain and lowered his head.

"M'excusez," he murmured.

Rose looked down at her mud-streaked legs. Beneath the filth, her fur was white. And it was glowing.

She knew then that she was on the goddess's business.

She slowed her pace and raised her head, glaring down at the man. Fumbling, he fished in his pocket and produced a key. He unlocked the manacle and made a show of releasing the boy, who bobbed his head at Rose and ran straight for his mother.

Rose stayed as she was. She didn't move until she heard the wheels of the rickety cart.

"*Merci, merci bien!*" the woman cried.

"Please don't hurt me," the guard whimpered to Rose.

What can I do to you? she thought incredulously.

"We won't follow them," he cried. "I swear it."

Rose was bemused. Hadn't Elise encouraged her to act with justice and mercy once she was a great lady? And so she had, in a most unexpected way.

I thank you, Artemis, she thought as the two men stared warily at her.

With a flick of her tail, she bounded away into the safety of the woods.

I have challenged men, she thought. *I stood firm. I did not run.*

Then she stopped glowing. Her white fur turned brown and she was an unremarkable doe again.

She went once more in search of her herd.

And as she traveled, Rose saw terrible things existing side by side with the lavish royal court: The strong oppressed the weak. The rich robbed the poor. The king's own guards bullied the peasantry; his tax collectors took more than they should. Too many fields were either completely barren or choked with weeds. Houses were tumbling down.

Did Jean-Marc not know? Did he not care? Why had he let these things happen? There was nothing of love in this.

Why did she need to ask how these things had happened? It was the way of the world of men. Similar things had happened to her. Perhaps deer lived a better life, closer to the perfection of the gods. Perhaps that was why Artemis loved them so.

Perhaps it would be best to remain in the forest and give up her human journey.

With that thought in mind, she looked for her herd.

TWELVE

As Rose continued her search for the herd, she came upon Reginer's *château* again. The royal newlyweds were visiting him, an occasion of joy.

"My brother, my dear brother," Desirée cooed as she stepped from the ornate litter that had transported her to Reginer's home. Ombrine had ridden in a second one. Jean-Marc sat astride a fine black steed.

Several guards and a lady-in-waiting came with them, carrying several jewel-encrusted goblets covered with golden saucers. From her vantage point, Rose could smell the liquid that two of the goblets contained: wine laced with sulfur and something else—something foul.

Rose watched until the front door closed. Then she trotted around to the side of the house, to the leaded glass window where her portrait still stood. She saw her reflection. She was a plain brown doe.

Reginer and his wife, Claire, made obeisance as Jean-Marc, Ombrine, and Desirée entered Reginer's studio.

"I brought you something to celebrate our reunion," Desirée said. Rose could hear her through

174

the window. At her signal, the lady-in-waiting glided forward with a tray. On it sat five goblets. Desirée lifted the tainted goblets and held them out to Reginer and his wife. "It's an old family recipe."

No! It's poison!

Rose clopped the earth and laid her ears flat. She bleated with fear. She couldn't stop herself. It was the deer part of her, reacting to danger. She pranced backward, away from the window. Her heartbeat roared in her ears. She smelled her own fear.

Danger, run! her deer self exhorted her. *Escape!*

She pictured the Marchands dead. Her terror escalated into panic.

What can I do? What can I do?

She whirled in a circle. She told herself to charge the window. She circled around and around, dizzy and out of control.

Artemis! she cried.

Then she bolted for the stable. She raced through the open gate and charged inside. A little dog bolted from its bed in the hay and faced her down, yipping in a high, piercing voice. The horses complained, chuffing and whinnying.

She harried the dog, darting toward it, bobbing her head. The dog yipped more loudly. The horses kicked at their stalls. They threw back their heads and neighed.

"For the love of the gods, what is wrong?" Reginer demanded as he strode into the stable. "What is this deer doing here?"

Relieved, Rose prepared to face him. Perhaps she could communicate with him, make him see who she was.

But as she turned, she smelled Desirée.

Rose darted through the stable and out the other door. She fled into the shelter of the trees and turned, watching as the Marchands' little dog burst out of the stable followed by Reginer.

"Monsieur Pierre," he remonstrated the pup as he scooped him up.

Desirée appeared, laughing; the dog growled at her and bared his teeth. He lunged as if he would tear out Desirée's throat.

"*Monsieur Pierre! Tais-toi!*" Reginer said. He huffed. "What was a deer doing in my stable?"

"Where is your stable boy? Your groomsmen?" Desirée asked.

"I gave them all leave to attend a feast with the king's horsemen," he said.

Scrabbling against Reginer's chest, the little dog lunged at her again.

"How ferocious," she drawled, amused. Rose's face still hovered above her own. Could no one else see the magic?

"I'll take him inside," Reginer said.

Reginer went back into the stable, leaving Desirée alone. Rose shrank back as Ombrine joined her. The two stood close together.

"Stupid dog," Desirée snarled. "I'll poison him too."

"Hush, my love," Ombrine said in a low voice.

"Let it go. We have what we want. You are queen and it seems that Rose is truly dead. No one has found her."

Desirée's smile sent chills down Rose's back. She had to close her eyes and look away, so that she wouldn't bleat or stamp the ground.

"Our god is great," Ombrine continued. "He saved us, did he not?"

"With all those birds," Desirée said. "Jean-Marc believes that Zeus sent them. Or Ares. I can't keep it straight. He's so gullible."

"The Marchands are not, however. The painter's been looking at us strangely. I think he suspects something." She sighed. "So it was with Laurent. He saw Celestine in me. He wanted her, not me. Murmuring her name, while I changed his filthy bed linens."

"There, there, Mother," Desirée said. "If not for him, we would not have met Rose. And it was she the king wanted."

"And he has her, thanks be to the God of Shadows." They put their foreheads together and smiled. "All that money she had squirreled away, rotten girl. It paid for our full acceptance into the Sorcerer's Circle. And now we can make men see us as we wish them to. Truly a dream come true for any woman."

"Yes, the king sees what he wishes to see," Desirée concurred. "But for how long, Mother? And what if others see something else? Someone else? Me?"

Ombrine laughed, low and clever and evil. "Why do you think I took that inventory? We'll take little things no one will miss and pay the Circle for more spells, more power. No one will touch us. Ever."

"No more starving. No more rags," Desirée exulted.

"I've been thinking that perhaps the god took Rose as payment. If so, he has favored us twice over. We are certainly blessed."

"*Oui*," Desirée said cheerily as she adjusted the cuff on her fine gown.

"Now, come, let's make sure Reginer Marchand drinks his wine."

No! Rose took an unthinking step toward them, panicking when she realized what she'd done. But they didn't see her.

With a second step, they would.

She caught her breath and forced herself to stay rooted to the spot.

Just then, Reginer's wife, Claire, came out of the stable. She was holding two of the golden goblets.

"Ooh, that dog," Claire said, with a moue of apology as she held them upside down and shook them, as if to illustrate her point. "He got loose and ran all over the studio! And I'm afraid he knocked over the wine."

Rose was startled. She remembered the two times she herself had dumped out Ombrine's proffered goblets. Was the goddess still at work?

"What a pity." Ombrine reached out and took the goblets. "We'll have to make some more."

"Indeed," Desirée said.

∽ ∽ ∽

The week of feasting ended and life for most in the Land Beyond went back to normal. But for Jean-Marc life extended into a state of bliss. He was a husband again and he hoped to become a father soon. In the evenings, he would return from his long day as king to find "Rose" standing at the balcony, gazing up at the stars with a faint smile on her face. In the mornings, the sun glimmered through her blond hair and dusted her creamy skin with gold.

With the queen by his side, Jean-Marc resumed the custom of dining with his nobles. After the death of Lucienne, he had usually dined alone. Now jesters and acrobats came to court. Minstrels and troubadours sang of love in the greenwood. His life was full to bursting, just like his heart.

Of an evening, he would stroll alone by the reflecting pond and think about the journey his heart had taken. The early death of his mother, Queen Marie, had cast a shadow over his childhood, and Lucienne was the sunshine that turned dour youth to happy manhood. Then her death sent him to a land of utter blackness, and sorrow was the only house where Jean-Marc could lay his head. Grief became his sanctuary.

Then the Rose Bride knocked and called him back out into the light. It was blinding, this love, so bright it burned. He wondered if one day it would mellow like a blazing fire that finally banks, with coals that give off steady and reliable warmth. He couldn't imagine such a thing. His love was all-consuming.

One night, not long after he had first seen the little brown doe, she appeared beside the statue of Artemis. She gazed directly at him as if she had been waiting for him. He was charmed and moved, and for a moment, afraid that perhaps the goddess had sent her on an errand that would end badly for him.

She stood her ground, though she shifted her weight and flicked her tail. Her distress signals made perfect sense: He was a man and a hunter. She appeared to be alone and vulnerable.

"*Bon soir, ma petite,*" he said softly. He walked over to her, bowed, and greeted her. She took two faltering steps backward and made shallow keening noises. "It's all right. I won't hurt you."

She turned tail and bolted.

The next evening, he saw her again. She permitted him to come a little closer, but fear overtook her again and she disappeared into the trees once more.

On the third night, she stood immobile as he approached. Then, when he was perhaps ten paces away, she laid down her ears and made her little crying noise. He was touched by her fragility, her vulnerability, and for no good reason than that he wished it, he set himself to the task of winning her trust.

By the fifth night, he thought to bring her a gift. It was an apple, shiny and red. He took it from the large golden bowl of fruit in his council chamber. Kings ate their apples with knives and forks, and he considered asking a servant to cut it up for her. But she was not a lady, she was a deer, and so he simply tucked it into his pocket.

He held the succulent fruit out to her. She took a cautious step toward him, and another. At the last, she stopped, and gazed up at him.

"Take it," he urged her.

But she would not.

Disappointed, he turned and resumed his path beside the pool. Then he heard the clop of her hooves. He slid a glance over his shoulder. Her ears were down—she was still anxious—but she fell in beside him and walked with him, as if she were a wolfhound on a leash. He was quite amazed and very pleased.

He held out the apple. She blinked at it, but didn't take it.

He walked. She kept pace.

"How is it with you?" he asked her. Of course she didn't answer. He didn't expect her to. As if she had asked, he said, "It is very well with me. I think you know why." He smiled. "I'm very much in love."

She made no response and they continued their stroll. After a time he said, "It's a wonder to wake up beside a wife again. I'd forgotten what it was like."

After that, they walked on in companionable silence. The doe was skittish, but she didn't flee.

He resolved that by the next full moon, she would take something to eat from his hand.

And so it became a ritual for them. Rose would wait for sundown, and Jean-Marc would appear. He always came alone and he brought her an array of tempting delicacies: apples, cabbages, carrots. After a few evening strolls, he took up the habit of bringing along his lute, which he would strum as they walked.

Mostly he spoke in raptures of his deep love for the queen. Then, over time, he began to discuss affairs of state and the doings of the court.

"My eyes have been closed for so long," he confessed. "I've let things go. I haven't provided for my people. I was so lost in my sorrow and then in my joy. No wonder Sabot was on me to marry. I wonder at the restraint he showed. He should have shaken some sense into me and made me see how completely I had lost the love of the people. The Pretender could never have taken such advantage if I had been a popular king."

He cocked his head at her. "Now that I've had a chance to gather my wits, I see the possibilities for change. I can improve the lot of my people and their children. And speaking of children . . ."

Her heart stopped beating. She faltered. *No, not with her*, she thought. She stared at him, smelled him. A child would seal them together. It was the way of things. Once that happened, all hope was dashed.

What hope? she chided herself. *Artemis has made you into what you are. She allowed him to marry Desirée.*

". . . my sister-in-law is going to have a baby," he finished.

Relief made her stumble. Claire and Reginer were to have a child. So they were well . . . so far.

And as for Jean-Marc . . .

It is not too late, she thought. But he had married her. He was bound to her by the gods. *He was tricked. . . .*

"Perhaps it will go that way with Lucienne and me," he said. She blinked at him and he blushed. "I meant to say Rose. Rose is my wife. Lucienne . . . died." He sighed and rested his chin on his chest. "At least, I think she did. You see, my new wife looks exactly like her. And I have thought . . ." He trailed off, gazing at the spires and turrets of his palace.

His voice fell to a choked whisper. He didn't look at her and his words came out diffident and uncertain, as if he felt that he was taking a risk.

"If indeed you are an envoy from Artemis, can you please tell me, is she Lucienne magically restored to me?"

Then and there, her hopes of love shattered. Monsieur Sabot had so much as told her that Jean-Marc had searched for her because of the resemblance. But to hear him say that it was Lucienne he still wanted, to hear the longing in his voice, and the wish . . . it hurt her more than she could ever have anticipated.

"Come," he whispered.

She gazed up at his dark eyes, his strong chin. Would he come to love Desirée for herself in time? Would Ombrine and Desirée bewitch him into thinking that he did?

She followed him and then they crossed into a

courtyard. Paper lanterns and festoons hung from the pomegranate trees. Lutes and tambours played and masked folk in fancy dress toasted each other with tankards. A peacock swayed past in all his glory. Monkeys giggled and capered in the trees.

"We're celebrating Reginer and Claire's new happiness," he said.

"Your Majesty, have you a new pet?" a man asked. He was dressed in soldier's gear, but he wore a half-mask above a beard braided with ribbons.

"Indeed," Jean-Marc replied. "I suppose I do." His voice was warm enough, but Rose smelled tension on him. It was getting stronger. It was becoming difficult for her to remain beside him. The fear pushed her animal instincts to the limit, ordering her to flee. But the woman she still was wanted to remain by Jean-Marc's side.

Jean-Marc stopped for a moment and she followed his line of vision. They were nearing a domed building fronted with columns. On a rise beyond it, a flame burned in a stone bowl.

Jean-Marc took a torch from a sconce in the stone wall and opened a door beside it. He said to Rose, "Follow closely, little one. There are steep stairs."

He spoke true. She walked down the sharp stone incline very carefully, her hoofs clacking, the noise echoing against the buffeting flame of his torch. His tension grew. On the last stair, he paused.

And then he walked into the dark, low room lined with sarcophagi, all of them topped with women lying in repose. This was the final resting place of queens, she guessed.

He knelt before the one in the center of the room. *"Et voilà,"* he whispered reverently. "If you have seen my present queen, you can see why I'm asking Artemis my question."

She drew up behind him and looked over his shoulder.

The room spun. Rose swayed. It could not be.

It could not be.

A painting was one thing. But the marble image was identical to Rose in every way. The arch of a brow, the shape of her nose—she searched for something that was different. There was nothing. She and the figure were closer than twins. They were the same woman.

It could not be.

Along the side of the alabaster, the name LUCIENNE had been cut into the stone. Rose read it three times to make certain it didn't say her own name.

She turned away, thinking that she understood the king a little better. If she had the chance to meet her mother's double, or Elise's, or even her father's, she would dare much to make it happen. If he had loved his wife half as much as she loved those whom she had lost, then she pitied him.

But she also knew straight down to her soul that whether he was married to Desirée or to her, Rose, it didn't matter. Maybe that was why Artemis had permitted Desirée to steal her appearance and changed her into a doe. To spare her from such a marriage. What would it be like to wed a man who saw you only as the most perfect of replacements? To know for a certainty that the best you could hope for was to ease the pain of true love's death?

Her purple roses had promised that she was loved. What Jean-Marc sought in marrying her was not love at all. It was comfort.

She was dashed. Bleating, she turned and headed for the stairs, her hooves making a terrible noise. Jean-Marc rose and called, "Wait! Stop!" but she couldn't. Human free will was not in command of her; her deer self knew she had to get out.

Danger.

For there is no greater danger to a human being than the breaking of one's heart.

Rose escaped from the mausoleum and dashed out into the festive courtyard. Panicking, she bleated and a portly man dressed like Dionysus, lord of wine, said, "For the love of the gods, look! Where's my bow?"

"Let's catch her! We'll have venison for breakfast!" shouted another, costumed like Poseidon, god of the sea.

Rose dodged them easily. They were both very drunk. But as she darted through the crowd, she caught sight of another man, standing distant, and her blood ran cold. He seemed to be made all of shadows and he was watching her. A dark bird perched on his shoulder. He seemed very like the dark figure she had seen with Ombrine and Desirée back at the *château*.

"By the gods!" a woman dressed like a princess shouted as she staggered toward Rose, obscuring her view. She was holding a cup of wine and a piece of cake. "Is this someone's tame doe?"

Then the woman swayed out of Rose's field of vision.

The shadowy man was gone. And as before, Rose wondered if she had imagined him.

"*Attends!* Wait!" she heard Jean-Marc calling behind her. She put on a burst of speed and raced through the courtyard, dodging the revelers.

Then she smelled her herd and crashed into the undergrowth, where she found them waiting for her. They ran away with her, deeper into the woods, where it was dark and she could no longer hear music. Each one in turn nuzzled her, and she bleated plaintively. They could not know she was weeping, but she was.

Then the king of the herd nickered and led her to a purple rosebush, which whispered, "*You are loved. You are loved.*"

Not by him. She pawed the ground and bobbed her head.

She gazed from one to the other with her large brown eyes, bleating *whew-whew-whew.* They pawed the earth in return, and the king buck cocked his head at her as if to say, *I will make you the queen of the herd. Give me your leave and it is done.*

So perhaps the one who loved her most was not a man at all. Perhaps Artemis had changed her into a deer so that she would be truly loved. Who could know the twists and turns her path would take? Her life had been so tumultuous already. Perhaps living out her days as a deer would give her peace.

Perhaps the love the goddess offered was not human love. Perhaps that was too imperfect, for all people were flawed. They were defined by their wounds unless they healed them. Their broken hearts weighted them down: *My love is a meager portion and I must dole it out carefully. I cannot dare to love like a god, because my love feels so limited and I am so afraid of the pain love has already given me.*

Jean-Marc was wounded thus. He carried his broken heart like a chain around his ankles. It made him stumble. But deer could run and gallop and canter. Perhaps that was why Artemis loved them so. They were free.

A wounded heart was a prisoner.

The roses told her that she was loved. That meant that someone loved her, knew how to love.

And if the sad king had ever known how, clearly he had forgotten.

Perhaps that's why I'm here, she thought. *I've been transformed, as I was told I would be. Have I been sent to help him on his journey to the light?*

THIRTEEN

Reginer and Claire moved into the palace so that Claire could be nearer the court physician during her time of confinement. Rose longed to go to her half brother, but she was afraid. Rose didn't know what sort of hold the Severine women had on him. They had managed to offer him wine again. Many times.

Jean-Marc declared a period of mourning for the lost Desirée. The real Desirée paraded in her black veils and dresses, weeping as if she were truly bereft.

Rose didn't know if Jean-Marc told Desirée of his twilight rendezous with the doe at the reflecting pool, but she did on occasion overhear others gossiping about a night when the king had walked with a little deer who followed him like a dog. It became the occasional topic of conversation. Rose's instincts told her that it would be safer for her to stay away. Out of sight, out of mind, and out of conversation; so she remained in the woods, watching Jean-Marc from afar. She longed to smell him, feel the heat of his body, but she stayed well away.

In that time, the king buck courted her. He brought her succulent berries and tasty pieces of bark. He showed her how to find fresh water. He nuzzled her face and her flanks, releasing scent that told of his desire for her.

You are loved, the purple roses promised.

As for Jean-Marc, he came to the pool every night, turning his head this way and that, searching for her. Watching from afar, her heart beat faster as she saw how disappointed he was. After a few evenings, he stopped bringing his lute. He simply completed his circuit around the pool and walked back to the castle.

A few evenings more and he began to leave presents for her at the feet of Artemis: apples, grapes, cubes of sugar. She took them at the first brushes of dawn when there was no chance he was waiting for her. She knew he would be asleep, beside his wife.

As the days and nights wore on, Rose's deer self crowded out her human self. She found herself forgetting how to think in French. She saw images in her mind of Jean-Marc, Reginer, and the Severines instead of thinking about them in language. Then even the images shifted, and she saw things from a forest creature's point of view—immediate and in front of her: Food. Water. Predators.

A mate.

Memories dissolved. In the fleeing moments when she still thought like a person, she remembered that because of a wish, Artemis had sent her on a journey. She couldn't imagine that the Fates had woven a tapestry designed to turn her into a deer. Artemis could have done that in an instant.

Then she thought of Desirée and Ombrine, who became harpies when their friends abandoned them. Solitude had changed them. Their hearts had hardened from misuse. Could it be that she was becoming a deer because she had no human contact?

No contact with Jean-Marc?

"*Où?*" he called. "Where are you?" Sometimes she thought she heard an owl and sometimes she heard Jean-Marc.

The buck pressed his suit, and one night her deer body wanted him in return. Rose was alarmed; she darted away from him. He pursued her through the bracken into a silvery meadow and then beneath the statue of Artemis itself.

Galloping up beside Rose, the buck stopped, panting, and nickered at her. Then he followed her line of vision and gazed up at the statue. He stared at it for a very long time. Then he dipped his magnificent rack of antlers as if in submission to a will greater than his own. He looked at Rose, turned away, and trotted back into the woods. Rose had no idea what, if anything, had passed between the goddess and him. When she herself returned to the forest, he stared at her with naked longing, but he did not approach her. Her deer mind understood that he was waiting for permission to court her and from now on, he would leave her alone until he had it.

Then and there, she realized that she had a choice to make—life in the forest or life on the unknown path the goddess had laid out for her. She needed to make it soon or else she would no longer have the human capacity to do so. But she was afraid. To cease all the toil and worry that came from being human . . . or to love. Jean-Marc was a love that could only end in sorrow . . . as so much of love seemed to. Why love at all, if it was not returned and if it died?

"That is what you are to learn," said a breeze.

She struggled with the decision. Her life had been so sad and difficult. She wasn't at all certain that what Artemis wanted for her was good to obtain. The gods could be cruel and capricious.

But it was not of the goddess she was thinking. Obeying her will was not the real choice. She loved him. Her love for Jean-Marc filled her with fear, but it was there and it was real.

And so, she chose.

And the herd left all at once, the does turning their brown eyes to her and whispering *adieu* in their nickering, bleating deer language. The lead buck with his magnificent antlers stood on a hillock as his subjects progressed past him, staring at Rose.

Then he too, melted into the night.

There was a full moon, and she let it guide her to the pool and to Jean-Marc. The moonlight glowed on his dark hair as he paused beside the statue of Artemis, casting highlights of midnight blue among the black strands. It had been washed with rosemary and lavender and she breathed in the mingled fragrances.

After a flutter of panic, she gathered up her courage and stepped into the moonlight. She watched him lift his chin and blink, as if he sensed her approach. He turned his head; at the sight of her, his face lit up.

"*Bonsoir*," he said, his voice hushed. "I thought you had gone forever."

She blinked at him. She had forgotten the rhythms and cadence of human words. Thoughts poured into her mind, thoughts anchored down with words. At that moment, she felt herself more woman than animal, and she had no way to tell him how overjoyed she was to see him. She danced sideways, then rose on her hind legs and pawed the air. The pads on her hooves released scent. It mingled with his odor and became something new. Fragile and powerful, soothing and exciting.

"I think you're glad to see me, too." His tone was amused and tender.

She wanted to ask him questions. How had he been faring? Was Claire big with child? Was Reginer safe? Was *he* safe?

He wouldn't know the answers to all her questions, but if only he would speak, she would know volumes. Deer could absorb a hundred telling details by smelling an object—whether other deer had been by, if there were predators, if food was plentiful. So it was, she now knew, with the way a person said a single word. She thanked Artemis for that knowledge.

"This is for you." He pulled a purple rose from his doublet. "Reginer's wife planted some cuttings and they have blossomed. These roses brought my wife to me. They're the most precious things I have."

For a moment all she could do was breathe in the heady aroma. It swirled around her like a caress against her cheek and she shut her deer eyes tightly against a tide of emotion. She had missed him more than she realized. Her heart had ached for him.

As with the time she had run wildly in search of him, now she felt her body reacting beyond her control. She trotted up to him and took the rose from his hand. Her velvety muzzle pressed against his knuckles. She had touched him, finally.

It brought her intense human delight.

"*You are loved,*" the roses assured her.

"*Et voilà,*" the king said. "There. At last."

She wasn't sure what he meant. She didn't eat the rose, tempting as that was. She placed it at the feet of Artemis and looked back up at him. She wished he had brought another, so she could take that from him too.

Yet when he stretched out a hand to pat her, she recoiled. She couldn't stop herself.

"*M'excusez,*" he said, lowering his arm. "Shall we walk?"

He half turned and she trailed behind him. She was overwhelmed. Her ears lay flat and she panted, but she forced herself not to run. He said to her, "It's all right. I won't hurt you."

The words shimmered like a dream. The calm sound of his voice never wavered. Whether she listened with doe or human ears, his soothing tone eased her jangled nerves.

She glided to his side. He regarded her for an instant and then he sauntered along. She watched his movements with deer eyes. He could be a predator, but at the moment he was at rest.

They walked together along the edge of the reflecting pool. He picked up a stone and dropped it in. She studied the sunset-tinted eddies and whorls. His profile was strong and sharp, his bearing noble. She thought of the elegance he must live in, the luxuries Desirée was enjoying as his wife and felt a stab of envy.

The water darkened. A wind ruffled Jean-Marc's hair. The days were growing shorter and winter was on its way.

In a quiet voice Jean-Marc said, "I'm sorry something spooked you in the mausoleum. I don't know what it was. Did you smell death?"

She gazed up at him. He cocked his head. "Perhaps I was wrong about the Rose Bride. The queen has been out of sorts lately. Sometimes I'm surprised at the way she speaks to the servants."

Rose held her breath. Was the magic wearing off at last?

"I think it's jealousy," he continued.

She stumbled, her hoof clicking against a rock. He didn't appear to notice.

"Claire—that's her sister-in-law—is growing very big with child. But Rose has yet to conceive. It must be difficult for her to see another's joy."

Several emotions washed over Rose, all at the same time. She looked down at her own reflection, a silhouette cut out of emerging stars.

"Still, near the end, Lucienne had many bad days, but she . . ."

A chilly breeze wafted over them both. Jean-Marc raised his face to the wind. A leaf fluttered past like an autumn fairy.

". . . she was always kind."

His voice was hoarse and his eyes were shiny with unshed tears. She listened to the anguish in his voice. He missed her. He loved her still. Desirée hadn't replaced her in his heart.

She couldn't help the tiny flame of happiness that flared inside her.

He did not blink and one of the tears spilled onto his cheek.

"The priest told us that we would have a son and he would heal two broken hearts. But our son died. And my heart was buried with them, in the darkness."

He set his jaw. "If I had been a more savage ruler, I would have killed that priest. More savage, or less afraid of the god he served. *My* god." The last he spoke without bitterness. She approved and understood. In the traditions of the times, it was wise to tremble before the divine.

She wanted to tell him that she, too, was puzzled by the actions of the gods. She didn't understand why everyone who loved her had been taken from her. Nor why Jean-Marc had entered her heart, despite the fact that she knew he would never love her for her own sake.

Yet I am alive, she reminded herself. *It's clear that Ombrine and Desirée would have had me dead. And because they can't see me, they think they succeeded.*

In silence, the pair continued their progress around the pool. She knew he would leave when they reached his starting point and she felt a deep pang.

All too soon they were there.

"It's late. I will be missed." He moved his hand as if to pet her, then stopped himself. *"Adieu."*

Don't speak of me to her, she begged him. But of course he couldn't hear her.

She watched as he walked toward the castle. Darkness closed over him like the cover of a book, and she returned to the forest, where she slept alone by her rosebush, trembling in the night.

When Jean-Marc returned to the palace, he found Claire Marchand waiting quietly for him in the shadows, a cloak hiding her condition from polite society. When he saw her, she stepped forward, attempting a curtsy although she was so big with child that it was beyond her.

"Non, non," he said gently, leaning forward and taking her wrists. "Is aught amiss? Your husband, is he well?"

She caught her breath. "I am not sure, Your Majesty." She twisted the edge of her shawl. "I beg of you, sir, please let me speak to you honestly without fear of punishment." She swallowed hard. It was clear she was very frightened.

"*Alors*, what is it?" he asked. "Come to our apartments. I'll have some wine brought."

"*Non, s'il vous plaît*," she said in a rush. She closed her eyes and shook her head. "I shouldn't have come. Forgive me, sir." She bobbed at the knees.

"Claire," he said, "I give you my word that you may speak to me honestly."

She took a deep breath. "Reginer says that Her Majesty's appearance seems to have altered in some way. He can't explain it, but he says that when he compares her face to that of the portrait that he painted, it is different."

The king considered. "Perhaps over time, he has come to observe her more closely and sees that he didn't quite capture her likeness." He chuckled. "Such are artists."

"*Oui*, that's what I said to him as well. But he insists that she has changed." She exhaled. "There. I have said it."

That gave the king pause. Hadn't he just said as much to his little pet doe?

"In what way?" he persisted.

She spoke in a rush. "Her hair and eyes are darker. Her features sharper. He even thinks that she's taller."

"Indeed? She's growing? What a miracle." When

he realized how upset Claire was, he grew more serious. "Pray continue."

She licked her lips and touched her swollen belly. "It was said that the Pretender looked exactly like your father in his youth. But I saw his body after it was brought in from the battlefield. He looked nothing at all like His Majesty. Perhaps his appearance was changed in a similar way...."

"Are you trying to tell me that you believe the queen is using magic to appear like my dead wife?"

She shook her head wildly, her face pale. "I have not said so. *Je vous en prie*, I have not."

He understood her terror. Charges of sorcery against the queen of the realm were a serious matter indeed.

"You have not," he assured her.

There was a fluttering of wings in the eaves above their heads. It sounded like a bat to Jean-Marc; Claire took it as her cue to leave.

"My husband doesn't know I came to see you," she said. "Please don't tell him. He would be angry."

"It stays between us," Jean-Marc promised her. "I don't take it amiss."

"*Merci. Merci bien*," she said feelingly. He waved off another awkward attempt at a curtsy and took his leave, bemused and thoughtful. What a strange conversation, and how ... unsettling.

Desirée was waiting for him in their private sitting room. A fire crackled in the hearth. The draperies were pulled back from the balcony, and he thought he saw a large bird flit across the moon as she turned. In her hand she held a steaming goblet.

She brightened and said, "Well met, my love. I was worried about you."

He took the wine. "I always go out walking this time of day. To sort my thoughts."

"You have much on your mind." Her voice was warm and sympathetic. She looked down at the goblet and said, "I prepared this for you. I need to speak to you, if you would be so kind."

The word "kind" jarred him slightly and he felt a tiny jab of guilt over having unburdened himself to the little doe. He had made no mention of the creature and he wasn't certain why he kept her a secret. Perhaps because he had been indiscreet; he knew she might be an emissary of the goddess. The Rose Bride had been a gift, and if he was honest with himself, tonight he had been finding fault with her. It smacked of ingratitude.

Coupled with his conversation with Claire Marchand, it smacked of something else altogether.

He studied her face carefully. Her hair was still silver and gold; her eyes, the most arresting starry midnight blue. And he knew very well how tall she should be and so she was. Reginer was looking for trouble where none existed. Perhaps it was nerves caused by impending fatherhood.

Desirée sat down on a divan covered with soft furs, inviting him with a sweet smile to sit beside her. The goblet was steamy with mulled wine, and he took a hefty swallow. It went down easily, warming his bones. Purring like a cat, she wrapped herself around him, laying her head on his chest. He knew her. He knew she was his Rose Bride. He let the conversation with Claire slide away, like the other cares of his long day, and settled in with his wife.

"I can hear your heart," she said. Then she leaned back and gazed up at him. "Two hearts beat inside my body." She waited a moment for her words to sink in. "*Mon amour,* we are going to have a child."

He nearly dropped the goblet. He stared at her. Every bit of joy in him, every shred of happiness, froze, held. He was afraid to be happy. Afraid to let in her wonderful news.

"How do you feel?" he asked carefully.

Confusion furrowed her brow. "What do you mean? Did you hear what I said?"

"How do you feel?" As if in slow motion, he put the goblet down on a small ebony table at his elbow—or at least he thought he did. He had gone completely numb.

"*Oh,*" she said as if she understood his meaning. She cupped his chin, forcing him to gaze steadily into her eyes. "I'm well, Jean-Marc. And I'm strong. I will have this baby, and I'll be there to raise him."

Him.

He closed his eyes and drew her into his arms. He was terrified. He had lost her once before. He must not lose her again. "We must do everything to keep you safe. We must thank my Father Zeus." His voice broke. "And you must go to bed and stay there until the baby comes."

"Jean-Marc, my dear love. With you near, I am safe." She kissed his cheek. "I will be the mother of a king."

"*Oui*, and he will mend two broken hearts," he whispered too softly for her to hear.

"You're holding me too tightly," she protested.

"*Alors*," he murmured. Then he rose and scooped her up in his arms; the familiar mixture of joy and grief seeped into his veins as he carried her to her bedroom. He was more seasoned now and humbled by life. He knew she was waiting for evidence of his unbridled happiness. This was her moment of triumph as a queen. This was the beginning of her greatest journey, into motherhood.

"I am happy," he whispered. "I am."

"I know." Her voice was a little shaky. "I understand why you're nervous. Truly, I do."

"You are my treasure." He laid her down on her bed and cupped her hands underneath his chin. "This explains why you haven't been yourself lately."

"*Oui*. To add to it, I've been sleeping badly. I've been having nightmares," she confessed. Then, with great reluctance, she added, "I've been dreaming that someone is trying to harm my baby."

He prickled with alarm. "Tell me."

"I—I didn't know at first that I was with child," she murmured. "It was my mother who guessed. She overheard some of my ladies-in-waiting. There is a ritual in your court, where we are to appear before the priests after the runes are cast. But we have not done it."

"We were married so short a time ago," he said. "Less than three months. I didn't want you to feel pressured. So much has happened."

"Indeed, so much." She managed a weak smile as she laid his hand over her flat stomach. Tears glistened in her eyes. "In the dream, there is a shadow that leans over his cradle."

He tensed. "A man?"

"I can't be sure." She looked away. "One has heard that the kings of the Land Beyond outlive many wives."

His mouth dropped open. "You can't be serious. You can't imagine that I—"

"*Non, non, mon amour*," she said in a rush. "I meant only that some say the royal wives are cursed. That something is at work that takes us from our husbands. Something evil." Her enormous blue eyes searched his face. "Perhaps I am dreaming of that."

"We must investigate this," he said. His thoughts moved back to his conversation with Claire Marchand and the strange coincidence of Reginer's meeting with his half sister. It occurred to him that the court painter could have lied about who he was. Perhaps he wasn't a Marchand at all. How odd that he would never visit his father, no matter the rift. Apparently the man had died and Reginer had never heard of it. Wouldn't someone at the *château* have contacted him?

She moved slightly so he could settle in beside her. She rolled on her side and propped her head on her hand. Drawing a lazy swirl on his cheek, she said, "The followers of Artemis consult with wisewomen, as you know. May I have permission to send for one to help us with this matter?"

"Of course. I'll give you whatever you want." Lucienne had never asked him for anything. Maybe if she had, she wouldn't have died. He kissed her forehead and then her nose, and lastly, her mouth. She put her arms around his neck.

"What I want most is your heart," she murmured against his ear.

"That you have already," he replied. He lay down beside her. "Sleep, my love. I'll guard you through the night."

Yawning, Desirée stretched her arms over her head. Jean-Marc lay wide-eyed beside her, on alert. Finally she fell asleep, her soft breath tickling his neck.

Then he rose, closed the bedroom door, and leaned against it. His hands shook. He shouldn't have found fault with her. He had tempted fate.

He strode back into the sitting room and finished the wine. Then he went into his dressing room, threw on a heavy cloak, and grabbed up his sword. He pulled the hood over his hair and left the palace via the servants' stairway, which he used for privacy and to elude his bodyguards. The temperature had dropped and his blood chilled as he strode across the dewy grass.

He took no lantern; the moon was his guide. The statue of Artemis was gauzed in moonlight and he walked right up to it and fell to his knees.

"Goddess," he began, and he took a breath. It felt so wrong to speak to her directly. And he should be at the temple of Zeus, asking the priests to intercede on his behalf. But he didn't want anyone beyond the family to know that the queen was with child. Not immediately, not until she was further along. He would have to tell her that when she awakened.

If she dies, I will die, he thought. *I couldn't bear it again.*

Propelled by his fear, he got to his feet and half ran to the burial vault. He took a torch from one of the sconces in the courtyard wall, pushed open the mausoleum door, and made his way downstairs to Lucienne's tomb.

He held the flickering light over his head and gazed down on her serene features. So she had been, always, in life.

"Lucienne," he said, kneeling beside her sarcophagus. With his free hand, he clasped the cold hands. The floor was frigid against his knees. Perhaps the first frost of age was on him.

"Lucienne," he said again. He fell silent because he didn't know what else to say. And then almost like a whisper, he thought he felt her hand squeeze back.

The words poured out of him. "I am afraid. I'm afraid." He lowered his head. "I am the king. I am the favored of Zeus. But I'm afraid."

He thought he heard the flapping of wings, but that would have been impossible unless some hapless bird had followed him inside.

He got to his feet and went back toward his palace. On the way he stopped again at the statue of Artemis, to discover a purple rose lying at the goddess's feet. He looked left and right, wondering if the little doe had left it for him.

Bemused, he lifted the blossom to his nose and breathed in the heady perfume. Then he thought he heard a soft whisper, as if it came from the rose itself. Blinking, he listened. There was nothing. He pressed the blossom against his ear.

It was only the sighing of the wind.

FOURTEEN

After he returned from the tomb, Jean-Marc stretched across the bedroom door to guard the Rose Bride. He had bundled his heavy cloak beneath his head for a pillow and pulled one of the furs from the sitting room over himself to keep warm.

His men of the bedchamber arrived to bathe and dress him for the day. Then it was time to eat the morning meal with the queen. He went to their private sitting room, where the table was laid and the hot tea was poured.

But she did not come. Ombrine appeared with her apologies, explaining to His Majesty that her daughter didn't feel well. Seeing his alarm, she reminded him that women in the family way were often queasy in the beginning. He demanded to see her, but after a difficult night, she had finally fallen asleep. Ombrine counseled that it would be best not to disturb her.

"It's normal. Natural," she soothed. "If anything, it bodes well."

He passed the morning in meetings. When the sun reached its zenith, he checked on her again. She was awake and glad to see him.

"I was afraid for you," he confessed.

"My mother told me." She waved her hand and a serving girl appeared with a steamy goblet of wine. "Drink this. It's the same soothing brew that I am drinking." She indicated a half empty cup on the table at her bedside.

He took a sip. It was a little bitter and he stopped. She grinned at him and tapped the base with her fingernail.

"Drink," she urged. She lifted up her cup and took a healthy swallow.

He drank it all down. It was delicious. He had never tasted wine so flavorful. A wave of light-headedness made him clumsy as he handed the goblet back to the servant.

"It's marvelous, is it not?" she asked. "It's an old family recipe."

"Marvelous indeed," he replied.

Night. And Jean-Marc. He was carrying a purple rose.

He walked toward Rose slowly. She was shocked by the change in him. A streak of gray ran through his blue-black hair; his face was haggard and careworn. There were lines in his forehead and at the corners of his eyes, and he shuffled along like an old man.

"How is it with you?" he asked her. "Let us sit together tonight, eh? I'm weary and my bones ache."

Rose bleated her distress. He smiled at her faintly and said, "I'm just tired. Nothing else is wrong. The queen had nightmares again last night. She says that

I did too. That I awakened her with my shouting."

She tilted her head, listening.

"I don't remember them." He yawned. "I seem to be forgetting a lot of things."

She blinked. *You are in danger*, she wanted to tell him. Or so she believed.

She folded her legs and sat down beside him. He reached out his hand very slowly. She did not flinch. He rested it on her back. Warmth spread throughout her body and she rested her head on her hooves.

"I have come to treasure these evenings," he said. "By this pool with you, I seem to become someone new. Someone . . . I was on the way to becoming a long time ago."

Her heart fluttered. She understood. She felt the same.

"There's something between us, you and me," he continued. "I don't know how to explain it or what to call it. But I'm grateful for it. Your goddess was kind to send you to me."

They sat side by side. It was a cold night, but Rose was cozied by the king's body heat as if she lay before a fire. Absently he stroked her back with his fingertips. She exhaled, not with fear but with pleasure.

The moon rose. As one, they looked into the gauzy light, and the lines and tiredness melted away from Jean-Marc's face. He looked young and vigorous.

"*You are loved*," the rose on the ground whispered to her.

He reached under Rose's chin and scratched her

along her neck. She shut her eyes tight, his touch a wondrous gift.

When she opened them, he was staring down at her.

"Are you crying?" he asked. "Can deer cry?"

"*You are loved,*" the rose whispered.

Rose moved her head so that it lay on his knee. A tear did spill, soaking into her fur, but she didn't think Jean-Marc saw it. She knew then, for an absolute certainty, that she loved him. In these months by the pool, he had bared his heart to her, and his soul. He had shared his secrets and his past. He had told her about being a lonely boy and a lonely man and she heard how deep his wound ran. But despite all he moved forward as best he could, forward into the hope of being loved. He had what he wanted. He *was* loved.

By her.

He didn't know it. He might never. But the gift had been given.

And what of me? Rose thought. *Who is it, who loves me?*

The wind blew and the moon glittered. Around them, the phantom garden of Rose's childhood pulsed and faded, pulsed and faded. He didn't see it. But she did and as she looked, she saw Jean-Marc as a young boy, sitting by the fountain. He was crying and as his tears dropped onto the ground, they became the silvery stream.

In the damascene moonlight, Rose's mother glided among the hundreds of rosebushes, ethereal as a goddess. Her expression was one of gentle pity; her arms were filled with white petals.

"Let him know that he is loved," she murmured.

She raised them over the little prince's head and released them. They showered down on his head and shoulders like fairy kisses.

"*You are loved. You are loved. You are loved,*" the petals breathed.

The boy looked up in wonder. He held out his hands and smiled. Then he began to laugh.

The vision faded. The garden disappeared. Rose shifted her head on Jean-Marc's knee.

The cold wind blew. Clouds scudded over the moon. A shadow traced the ground, then vanished.

"Tomorrow the moon will be full," Jean-Marc said.

"*Oui,*" Rose replied, but the sound she made was a deer sound.

"I must go." He moved his hand away and she lifted her head from his knee.

They both stood.

"*À demain,*" Jean-Marc said to her. She bobbed her head.

Then each went their way in the moonlight.

When she returned to the forest, Rose tossed and turned. She missed the herd, and without the protection of others of her kind, she constantly jerked awake, scanning the darkness for predators.

Thus it was that she was awake when Ombrine and Desirée crept through the darkness. She rose unsteadily and darted behind a tree, watching. They wore black cloaks and carried lanterns. Behind the pair, a black shadow moved, with a bird on its shoulder.

Then a third woman, wrinkled and stooped, moved from the opposite end of their path.

"Hail sisters, well met," she said, raising her lantern. "My lord," she added, curtsying deeply before the shadow. It wordlessly inclined its head. "How goes the plan?"

Ombrine stepped forward. "It is as we feared. Le Noir"—she gestured to the bird—"has told us that the spell is weakening. Reginer Marchand has begun to see Desirée as she really is. Claire Marchand met in secret with the king. And he did not share this information with his queen."

"That's ominous," the old woman said.

"Or merely gallant," Desirée drawled. "He's like that."

The bird on the shadow's shoulder cawed. The crone cocked her head, listening to it. It cawed rapidly and fluttered its wings. The dark figure stood impassively as the bird continued.

"He has made a pet of a deer?" the old woman asked the bird.

Rose fought the urge to bleat with fear. Her ears flattened; her tail twitched. She willed herself to freeze.

"Something of a confidante." Ombrine sniffed. "Can you imagine?"

"I can," said the crone. "Surely it has occurred to you that deer are the subjects of Artemis? And Celestine Marchand was her Best Beloved. Or so I have read in the runes."

"And Rose was the Best Beloved of her mother," Ombrine said slowly.

"Can't this wait?" Desirée asked, yawning. "I'm cold. I want to go back to bed."

"Rose's body has never been found," Ombrine said to the old woman. "One assumes the Pretender's men killed her and left her to rot, but one cannot be certain. Tell me, Mother Hecate, this deer . . . follow me here. We have used a glamour to present Desirée to the king as Rose. Could Rose be enchanted so that she appears to be a deer?"

"That can't happen," Desirée objected. "That's just too strange."

"Of course it can happen." The old woman—Mother Hecate—shrugged her shoulders. "The Pretender used a glamour to appear as Henri's son. And the God of Shadows appears to us now as a figure of living darkness."

The three women turned to the dark figure and curtsied low. The silent figure inclined its head.

"You're new to the ways of sorcery," the old woman told Ombrine. "But you've achieved so much. For centuries, we've tried to form a Circle within the palace. We've never succeeded. We're so very close now."

"I've fed the king the new potion," Desirée said. "He can't remember anything from one night to the next."

Hélas, Rose thought. *They are poisoning him!*

"That is only a temporary measure. One that you must not continue long," Mother Hecate reproved. "If that idiot Sabot and the council decide that the king has lost his mind, they'll depose him and name a Regent."

"That would be me," Desirée declared. "That would be even better than queen!"

Ombrine laughed sourly and rolled her eyes. "You'd be a ripe target for assassination, *ma belle*. Better to let a man stand between you and a sword."

"Your position would remain far more stable with the king in place. And so would the Circle's." Mother Hecate reached into the sleeve of her robe. "I've prepared some incriminating documents that will falsely link Reginer and Claire to the Pretender. Conceal them in their apartment in the palace."

She handed Ombrine several sheets of parchment, one rolled up as a scroll. Then she reached into her other sleeve and pulled out a bag that reeked like carrion. Rose's eyes began to water.

"Put this in Jean-Marc's wine," she told Desirée. "He will be more suggestible. Whisper in his ear that the Marchands are traitors. He will hear you."

Ombrine grabbed the bag out of Desirée's hand. "I'll take care of these." She opened the drawstring and peered inside. "How much?"

"Two pinches," the crone told her.

"Let's whisper as well that his little pet doe is in on their scheme," Ombrine told Desirée.

"Well said," Mother Hecate said. "If she's a problem, she's taken care of. If she's not ... well, one less deer and who cares about that?"

Ombrine and Desirée tittered. Desirée bounced on her heels. "This is so much fun."

"Have a care," Ombrine said. "It was not 'fun' when we were starving to death."

Mother Hecate raised her arms toward the moon.

"Artemis stole the moonlight from you long ago, my lord," she said to the shadowy figure. "We promise you that we will continue to fight for your ascension. To that end, we promise you a firstborn."

Rose caught her breath as Desirée placed her hand over her stomach. She could not be with child. Not Jean-Marc's child.

"Does he suspect?" Ombrine asked Desirée.

"That I have lied about carrying another heartbeat?" she asked. "Never fear, I'll take care of that soon enough." She curtsied low to the shadow. "I will whisper to him of love. Then I will conceive, my lord, and give the babe to you."

Non, non, Rose thought. She ground her teeth together to keep herself from bleating. She longed to paw the ground.

"We must away," Mother Hecate announced. "The dawn is coming. The king will awaken and wonder where you are. You told him you've sent for a priestess, *oui?* I'll come with you and help you close the trap."

The four glided through the trees. Rose waited, her heart racing, to go to Jean-Marc and foil the plot, if she could . . . or to warn Reginer and Claire, if she couldn't.

∞   ∞   ∞

Two hours later, Jean-Marc paced as he waited for the results of the search of the Marchands' apartment. He had awakened from a clear vision of their treachery—a gift from the gods, surely, meant to protect the Favored Son of Zeus. His wife was overwrought from a vision of her own. Ombrine had come as soon as he had summoned her, and brought with her "the priestess of Artemis" he had given his wife permission to bring to the castle.

"I dreamed of a little deer," Desirée told Mother Hecate. "She creeps to the baby's cradle, and then she raises up on her hind legs and crashes down on top of him."

She burst into sobs. "And she kills him!"

"Mon amour, ma belle." Alarmed, Jean-Marc gathered her in his arms and held her against his chest. It couldn't be his little pet, could it? Impossible.

"It's a sign from the goddess. She is warning us." Weeping, she dug her fingers into his arms. "Someone in the court is practicing witchcraft against us."

At that moment, there was a knock on the door to their private rooms. Jean-Marc himself answered it, and Monsieur Sabot stood white-faced on the other side. In his hand he held a sheaf of papers.

"It is as you dreamed, sire," he said with a bow. "Documents showing that Reginer Marchand is not who he pretends to be. His name is Robert Bienville. The Pretender's spies discovered Rose

Marchand, and Bienville pretended to meet her by accident. Her Majesty is truly who she says she is. She is innocent of all of this."

He bowed in Desirée's direction. "But Bienville still plots His Majesty's downfall with the Pretender's cousin."

"By the gods, his death shall be hideous," Jean-Marc hissed. "*Merci*, Monsieur Sabot. I'll meet with you in the council chambers in ten minutes."

Monsieur Sabot bowed low, and left.

"Your Majesty, there is more," the old woman declared, reaching into her pocket and pulling out a handful of ivory tablets. "I have cast the runes. There is another traitor very close to you. I have been unable to discern his—or her—identity, but I can give you a mirror that will allow *you* to see who it is."

She reached into a black satin bag covered with white stars and pulled out a small hand mirror in an ebony lacquer frame. The mirror face was black as well, as if the silver backing had tarnished.

"By tonight's moon, look into this mirror, and you will see the traitor. There will be no mistake. You will see the guilty one."

"Here is more wine," Ombrine announced, carrying a fresh tray of goblets from a servant at the bedroom door. "Drink, my son-in-law. You have need of fortitude for the wild work ahead."

Grabbing a goblet, he drank the fragrant brew down in three swallows. Vertigo washed over him as he set the goblet back down on the tray.

ༀ ༀ ༀ

Night. Rose had tried all day to get close to the king, Reginer, or Claire. But none of them had come out of the palace and she couldn't find a way in. The guard had been doubled, tripled. Men in official robes came and went, murmuring together.

Monsieur Sabot strode out of the palace. Perhaps she could go to him, try to make him understand.

Monsieur Sabot nodded at a young pageboy holding a trumpet. The boy blew on the instrument and suddenly the yard was filled with armed men wearing the colors of the king. Some were running; a trio cantered through on horseback. Torches burned. Swords and axes caught the light.

"We can't find them anywhere," a man in a helmet said to a bearded man in a broad-brimmed hat. "They must have been warned."

The bearded man took off his hat and scratched his forehead. "I can't believe this. Someone is misinformed. Reginer Marchand and his wife are devoted to the king."

"The king himself denounced them," said the man in the helmet. "He's ordered their arrest. He's signed their death warrants."

"It's a pity then." He put his hat back on. "Well, we have royal orders to follow. King Jean-Marc has spoken and we must obey."

Rose reeled. She thought of Reginer, how devastated and terrified he must be. And Claire—

she had to be near the time of her child's birth.

And the God of Shadows had been promised a firstborn.

Non, she protested, but it came out as a bleat. She forced herself to silence and stayed well to the shadows as she slinked away.

A crier shouted, "Reginer and Claire Marchand, you are hereby charged with high treason! Throw yourselves on the mercy of His Majesty King Jean-Marc of the Land Beyond!" His voice echoed, as the voices of criers do.

Rose turned and fled.

Where could her brother be? She had to help him, had to hide him until she could find a way to reach Jean-Marc. She had to stop him from murdering the Marchands.

I should have tried harder when I had his ear, she thought.

She ran through the woods, bleating, calling for her brother. Wolves and boar shot from their lairs, eager to run fresh venison to ground. They gave chase; she clattered over rocks and splashed through streams. Branches slapped her face and cut into her sides. She started to slow and her enemies cut the distance in halves, in quarters.

Reginer? she called. *My brother!*

She ran, bleating, alerting more predators. The forest teemed with death. She kept going, kept running, searching everywhere for her family.

What can I do for them when I find them? It would be better to find the king.

"But you have lost Jean-Marc," a cold, sorcerous wind whispered in her ear. "He is ours now because of a wish. Your mother's wish."

I don't believe that, Rose thought.

Through the dark and the night, as the wolves howled and the boar slathered, she ran.

White-knuckled, Jean-Marc clutched the crone's magic mirror. The glass reconfirmed the three conspirators—Reginer, Claire, and the little brown doe. Of the three, the doe's betrayal cut the deepest. He had believed her to be a messenger of Artemis and he poured out his heart to her. He was humiliated.

Perhaps she *was* a messenger of Artemis. Perhaps Artemis herself had betrayed him. His Lucienne dead, his Rose threatened . . . perhaps the goddess needed killing too.

His wine goblet splashed against his doublet as he swayed before La Magnifique, his hunting horse. The riders were assembling. The king would lead the hunt for the treacherous deer.

Ombrine was dressed for the hunt, in riding clothes and boots. A huge dark bird sat on her leather gauntlet. She held out a goblet of wine to Jean-Marc and said, "Fortify yourself, Your Majesty."

He drank lustily. "By the gods," he said, "this is bitter brew." But he drank it down.

Then she turned her attention to Desirée, as

her litter approached. Lying on soft pillows, she had put on her bridal gown as a token of her love. When Jean-Marc's eyes met hers, a tear slid down her cheek.

"Please be careful. Come back to me and to our child."

"I'll come back to you," he vowed. He took another draw on his wine. Then he handed her the cup.

"To horse!" he cried.

The call went up.

"To horse! To horse!"

Miles from the castle, Rose found Reginer and Claire beneath the wooden bridge that spanned the river Vue. Claire was in labor and Reginer was frantic.

Wolves and boar swirled behind Rose like a living cape. *Reginer, I am your half sister, Rose,* she pleaded, as a black wolf pulled forward from the pack and flew at her. She smelled dead meat on its breath. Droplets of saliva sprinkled her fur.

It was about to go for her throat when her fur turned white and she began to glow. From head to hoof, she shimmered with magic, and Reginer gave a shout of surprise. He pulled his sword from his scabbard. He speared one wolf through the foot; another, through the heart. He cut down a boar, which squealed and thrashed until it died.

The rest ran off to await an easier catch.

"Do you come from Hermes?" he asked, dropping to his knees. "For the love of the gods, I pray you, help us. Our horses have run off and my wife is having our baby."

She said nothing, only nosed him aside so she could examine Claire. There was nothing she could do for her sister-in-law, so she bumped up against Reginer, hoping to give him comfort.

Horns, drums, and hounds exploded, and Rose sniffed the air. The fur rose on the back of her neck. She smelled at least a dozen horses. At least twenty men.

And Jean-Marc.

"They're hunting us," Reginer said. "I heard the herald. We're wanted for treason. I'm sure it's the queen's doing. I've had a feeling about her. She's an imposter. I know it."

You are right. She stamped the earth. She heard the swoop of the threshers as they smacked the bushes. The clamor of the drums. The baying of the dogs.

Horse hooves pounded. Horse tack jingled.

"*Reginer,*" Claire moaned, reaching for her husband. Her hair was damp against her forehead. "Our baby, our baby. I can feel it coming!"

"I pray you, help us," Reginer implored Rose. He fell prostrate before her. "I have been a loyal worshipper of Hermes for my entire life. *Je vous en prie*, reward my loyalty. Or if I must die, save my wife and child."

Artemis will save you through me, Rose told him. *Adieu, my beloved kinsman.*

She dipped her head in farewell and turned tail. She dashed into the bracken, directly for the hunters. She prayed to the goddess to keep her alive at least long enough to deflect the pursuit from Reginer and Claire.

The light faded from her body. She became a simple brown doe again. But her heart glowed like a comet.

Now I know true love. I know what it is. I know how it feels.

Overcome with joy, she ran to certain death.

"I'm on the scent!" Jean-Marc announced. Then the world wobbled and rocked and waves of dizziness made him grab the pommel of La Magnifique's saddle. He put his trembling hand to his sweaty forehead. He was shaky and ill.

"My son," Ombrine shouted to him. "How do you fare?"

Something is wrong.

He shook his head as if to clear it. Sharp pain throbbed behind his eyes and sliced into the back of his head. His stomach clenched.

"Keep riding," he gasped, gathering up the reins as he held on to the saddle.

She couldn't have heard him, but she spurred on her horse, thundering on ahead into the dark forest.

Another pain seared his eyes. *This is wrong.*

He pulled out the mirror and gazed into it. The little brown doe stared back as if she could see him.

She ran along the river, panting and bleating. He knew she was afraid.

Run, he told her grimly. Then his heart seized with the memory of the nights they had walked together, the secrets he had shared with her. His heart melted for an instant and he thought, *Don't let us catch you.*

With another seizure of his body, the thought was expelled from his mind as if he had spit rotten meat out on the grass.

Rose ran. Ombrine's bird of prey flew above her, cawing, announcing her position to the horsemen. She turned from the river and made for the woods. Alerted, the hounds bayed and charged after her. Horns and drums signaled the change in direction.

Away from the river Vue, away from the wooden bridge, Rose panted and bleated, losing track of her direction. She knew her hoof pads were dropping scent everywhere. The well-trained dogs would run her to ground. The best she could hope for was to divert them from Reginer and Claire before they ripped her to shreds.

She hopped over a branch, smacked into another. Her ankle cracked and she went down. Heaving on her side, she struggled to rise.

The monstrous bird circled, cackled, swooped down. It missed her and soared into the sky again, hovering like a kite, so that its mistress could get a fix on its position.

Rose got to her feet. Her front leg burned; when

she put weight on it, she thought she would faint from the pain. But she hobbled on, praying, always praying and wondering why the goddess was allowing this to happen.

"She's doubling back!" Ombrine cried, pointed at her circling bird.

The alert was sounded. The buglers and drummers announced another direction as the hounds bayed and looped back toward the horses.

Jean-Marc was drenched in sweat. Something inside him pulled at his stomach and pummeled his rib cage. It hunched inside him like a nightmare on the chest of a dreamer and it tried to take the reins. He wondered if Artemis was trying to thwart him.

La Magnifique thundered through the forest and back onto the manicured lawns of the castle. They rounded the battlements.

And then he saw her as she staggered from the trees to the right of the statue of Artemis. She was limping badly and her sides sucked in and out like a blacksmith's bellows. She fell to her knees, head drooping downward. With supreme effort, she forced herself back up to a standing position and dragged herself closer to the figure.

She looked over her shoulder at the chargers and the hounds. The archers in the party unhooked their bows and notched arrows. They took aim.

"Kill her!" Ombrine exhorted them. "Run her through!"

"*Non!*" Jean-Marc boomed. "I will do it!" He gestured to the lead rider. "Tell the buglers. The kill is the king's!"

The word was given. The archers put down their bows. The party split into halves as Jean-Marc galloped down the center. He remembered the night that Artemis had slain the Pretender for him and realized that he was facing her down now himself. If she had a mind to, she could let loose her stone arrow and kill him.

Something is wrong with me, he thought as his guts wrenched. His back felt as if someone were twisting it like a wet bedsheet. *Something is alive inside me. Something evil. Something dark.*

He steeled himself against the pain as he pulled La Magnifique to a stop. From the corner of his eye, he saw the Rose Bride's litter. Why had she come? He didn't want her to see this.

Concealing his agony, he dismounted. Then he pulled his sword and advanced on the little doe.

How could this happen?

Tears rolled down Rose's face as she fell before the statue of Artemis, Goddess of the Hunt and of the Moon. She heaved with exhaustion; she was cut and scratched. The king had run her to ground and she knew he meant to kill her. His face was grim; his battle sword was drawn.

She could not move.

"I do this for love," he declared as he raised his sword over his head.

How could that be? Love did not cut down. It never did. Hatred did, and grief. But love nurtured and protected.

At least Reginer and Claire would have a chance now. She had given that to them. Perhaps that was the lesson she was supposed to learn: that to be loved, one had to love first.

She raised her head and gazed up at Jean-Marc. She loved him. She loved what he could have become if he had learned how to love and not only to need. To give and not just to want.

She blinked at him. *Adieu*, she thought as the sun glinted off the thick, sharp blade.

"Do it!" Ombrine cried.

"Do it!" Desirée chorused from her litter. She was wearing Rose's bridal gown, and as always, Rose's face hovered above her own. But her eyes were black.

Jean-Marc looked in turn at Desirée and Ombrine. Ombrine was dismounting. Desirée climbed down off the litter. Together they converged on Rose and Jean-Marc.

Jean-Marc hesitated. As he gazed down at Rose, he grimaced. Sweat was rolling down his face and she realized he was in pain.

"Who are you?" he asked in an agonized wail. "Are you a sorceress? What have you been doing? What did you do to me?"

She bleated. She was terrified. Was this to be her end? Would he make it quick?

The sword wavered. His face changed. Angrily,

defiantly, he stabbed the sword tip into the ground.

"You wouldn't harm me," he declared. "You wouldn't harm my child. You couldn't."

Then he contracted forward with a groan. He began to retch; he gripped his head and moaned low and long. He fell to the grass and onto his side.

His men leaped off their horses and raced toward him. From her vantage point, Rose watched him writhe and groan. A trail of darkness escaped from his mouth, undulating as it rose into the sky.

Ombrine and Desirée reached Jean-Marc. Desirée grabbed his sword. It was too heavy for her; her mother wrapped her hands around Desirée's and together the two women rushed Rose.

"No!" Jean-Marc yelled from the ground. He forced himself upright and ran for his sword. But he was too far away and the two Severine women had the advantage.

As the tip of the sword touched Rose's throat, the statue of Artemis moved. Her chin raised, her eyes narrowed, and she pulled on her bowstring. She aimed and let her arrow fly.

It shot through the air like a falling star, like a comet. The assembly fell back, watching as it arched against the sun and plummeted toward the earth.

And though the arrow's trajectory made it impossible to accomplish, the stone arrow slammed into Desirée's chest and pierced her heart.

"*Maman*," Desirée whispered as Rose's features completely disappeared and Desirée's true face was revealed.

"What is this?" Jean-Marc shouted as he grabbed up his sword and pointed it at the pair.

A shadowed figured hovered behind Ombrine's shoulder, bent over as if to inspect Desirée's wound. Ombrine did not see it; nor did she see the large blackbird—Le Noir—perched on its shoulder. The bird lifted its beak to the skies and cawed.

As if summoned, a tremendous flock of large blackbirds burst out of a bank of clouds. Hundreds of them wheeled and shrieked, as they had on the day the Pretender had attacked the coach. But in that case, they had protected Ombrine and Desirée Severine. Now they shot down toward them like more arrows of Artemis.

As Ombrine screamed and flailed her arms, the birds descended on her, catching up her hair, her clothes, her fingers. They clung to Desirée like ravening beasts as well.

Then they rose up, up into the sky, bearing mother and daughter with them. Ombrine struggled, shrieking, *"Au secours! Au secours!"* until they flew so far away that she became a dot and then nothing.

Nothing at all.

Rose stared at the vast sky, feeling sorrow and anger rising from her shoulders and flying away into the heavens with her evil stepmother and stepsister. Perhaps the God of the Shadows had taken a first-born in payment after all.

She nearly floated into the sky herself. They were

well and truly gone and she was free. She was safe.

For a moment, she was overcome. She had gone through so much, and had endured, come through changed, certainly. And yet she had been on guard for so long that she didn't know how to let go of her fear. So it tugged at her heart a while longer; then it too, flew away.

"*You are safe now,*" a breeze whispered against Rose's ear.

Jean-Marc and all the other hunters looked from the sky to her. No one spoke. No one moved. A horse nickered. A dog barked softly.

"*You loved boldly and freely in the face of certain death. Your love is true and you know that it is true. You know love for what it is and what it is not. You are truly Best Beloved of the goddess, and I charge you, Rose Marchand, to accept nothing less than true love from one who would walk in the garden with you. For while men themselves may be imperfect, they can strive to love perfectly. When one struggles to love in this way, one is a lover worthy of you. Else, you must bid him adieu.*"

Rose bobbed her head. She understood.

"*Then I release you from your enchantment.*"

And in that moment, that instant in the sunshine, Rose sent out a thought for the king of the deer and wished him well. She could almost hear his answering nicker, wishing her the same. Then the deer that had been Rose Christine Marchand vanished. Rose the woman stood before Jean-Marc in the black rags she had worn when she'd left the *château*.

"*Mademoiselle,*" Jean-Marc breathed, racing

forward and gathering her in his arms. "What magic is this?"

She allowed herself a moment in his embrace, shutting tight her eyes. Then firmly but gently, Rose moved away. No magic then. She was who she was.

"Artemis, I thank you," she whispered as she knelt before the statue.

Jean-Marc knelt beside her. Then one by one, all the huntsmen bowed before the Goddess of the Hunt and of the Moon, a woman's goddess.

Rose was given a horse—she refused to ride Ombrine's—and she guided Desirée's litter to the wooden bridge. There they found that Claire had given birth to a son, whom she named Laurent. As sister and brother met as humans for the first time, weeping with joy over love's triumph, mother and babe were put onto the litter.

Reginer rode Rose's horse, Rose seated behind him with her arms around his waist. She laid her head against his back, unable to staunch her tears of happiness.

As they rode back to the castle, Rose told Reginer everything that had happened since the royal coach wheeled away from the *château*. Jean-Marc kept pace beside them on his magnificent hunting horse. His face was ashen and he remained silent.

They dismounted at the palace, Reginer first, then he lifted Rose down.

"I thank the gods that all has ended happily," her

half brother said, embracing her tightly and kissing both her tearstained cheeks before he excused himself to be with his wife and new child.

After Rose visited little Laurent and his parents, she bathed and changed into some warm clothes—a deep scarlet velvet gown, one of the many dresses that had been made for Desirée. Her blonde hair was braided and coiled on top of her head, and she was left alone with Jean-Marc in a small private sitting room. Desirée's scent permeated the room. So did a foul stench of black magic—sulfur, wormwood, and herbs Rose didn't know.

"All has not yet ended happily for us," Jean-Marc said as he faced her. He too, had changed his clothes. He wore purple, the royal color. "If I understand you, I married Desirée instead of you. She took your visage in order to deceive me. She convinced me that it was she I loved."

Rose hesitated. Then she swept a deep curtsy and said, "With all due respect, Your Majesty, you also deceived yourself. You were never in love with her."

It was his turn to pause. "I grant you that."

"You don't know how to love," she said frankly. "You know how to need."

His dark eyes met her deep, starry blue ones. He swallowed hard at the hard truth she spoke. Then he swept a deep bow and said, "*Tu as raison.* I can learn to love. You know that I can. You know me better than anyone on earth. I have told you things I've never told another living soul." He sounded almost desperate and she knew he was terrified of being alone again.

Rose put her hand in his and his smile lit up the room. Her heart broke again because she was not his true love. How many times had it been broken?

Not so many that true love couldn't heal it.

But Artemis was right: True love *alone* could heal it.

Pursing her lips together to force away her tears, she gave his hand a gentle squeeze.

"If you can, then someday you will," she replied.

Rose turned to the fire and warmed her hands.

If she would turn blind eye to the fact that Jean-Marc didn't love her as he should—with a strong, giving love, she would be a queen. After all the privations of her life, living such a life held its temptations. But as she gazed into the flames, she heard at last her mother's wish:

"Let her know that she is loved with a love that is true and will never fade as the rose petal fades. If she knows that, it will be all that she needs in this life. A woman who is loved is the richest woman on earth. Knowing you are loved is the safest of harbors. True love never dies. It lives beyond the grave, in the heart of the beloved. If she knows she is loved, she'll be rich and safe for all her days."

"What you offer me is not true love," she finished as she turned around. "And my goddess—and I—decree that I can live with nothing less."

FIFTEEN

Why did Rose Marchand look like Princess Lucienne? Perhaps the proper question was, why did Princess Lucienne look like Rose Marchand? What caused the death of a princess, a wound so great that it brought her husband to his knees? What promise did the runes of Zeus foretell when they said that Jean-Marc's son, Espere, would mend two broken hearts?

After Rose told Jean-Marc that his love was not true, he set out to prove her wrong. He wooed the Rose Bride. He installed her in a sumptuously decorated apartment next to the Marchands. Claire's seamstresses created a wardrobe fit for an empress.

One day, as she adjusted the hem of one of Rose's new gowns, Claire said, "I have an older dress, madame, that seems as if it were made for you. I purchased it from a countess, who bought it from a widow. I once tried to offer it to your stepsister, but her mind was fixed on what she did and didn't want, and so I never brought it to her. May I show it to you?"

"*Bien sûr,*" Rose replied.

And of course it was the magnificent pink birthday gown. The layers were tattered here and there, and in places, the golden embroidery had dulled. But of a piece, it made the other seamstresses gasp, and Rose's heart swelled with gratitude that her gown had been returned to her at last. It was like seeing her parents one more time.

"This was my dress," Rose told her. "My birthday gown." As she explained what the dress meant to her and what she had done to lose it, she gazed at it with longing. "I was smaller then. It won't fit now."

"I'll adjust it," Claire promised.

Jean-Marc continued to press his suit. Rose's food was the most delectable, her wine, rare and excellent. He showered her with gifts. He serenaded her. He wrote her poetry.

But Rose knew he still didn't didn't love her. He was still too deeply hurt by what had happened before their paths had crossed. Perhaps the gods had willed Lucienne to look like her so that the tiny flame inside his soul would take in the air of hope and grow brighter.

And so, while she was kind, she did nothing to return his love—although, of course, she loved him with all her heart. Of a night, she would walk the balcony of her apartment and gaze up at the moon. Sometimes she wanted him so much that she thought of begging Eros, the god of love, to shoot Jean-Marc with an arrow. But the gods had done enough.

A month passed and then a year. Jean-Marc did all he could to buy her heart, hunting the coin as her father had done. When he came to her rooms, he would find her dandling baby Laurent on her knee. At the first, he would ask a nurse to take the baby so that he might speak with Rose alone. Then one day, as Rose held the little Laurent, the sunshine glowed in the babe's eyes just so, and Jean-Marc saw how much he resembled his aunt. And he was taken by surprise at the pain in his heart.

I was a child once, he thought. *And I lost Marie, my mother, the one I loved.*

I had a child, and he is gone.

He didn't realize that he had just brought the deeper wound into the light. The death of his wife was a tragedy, the loss of his mother a terrible blow, but the loss of his child had defined him. Running beneath everything he had become, a dark, secret wound had stunted the growth of his heart. He hadn't known it. Such things were of the realm of the gods and the softer hearts of women. Or so King Henri had taught his motherless heir.

But he faced his terrible secret: *I failed to bring life to my son. I failed him and I lost him.*

That night, he had a dream.

Marie, queen of the Land Beyond, mother to the infant Crown Prince Jean-Marc, walked in a rose bower. Purple roses grew in waves and rows, curtains and canopies. White roses released fragrance; red, orange, and yellow roses formed tapestries hanging from the trees. In her arms she carried her newborn son, and tears streamed down her cheeks.

"I will not see your first week," she told her sleeping child. "I will not be there to calm and soothe and love you. I will not be there to teach you how to love."

The roses shimmered and scintillated as she glided through the fairy bower. She said, "Our god is Zeus, a god of men's hearts. He calls them to action. He calls them to fight and to protect. But he doesn't call them to love."

Moonlight streamed down from the heavens and Marie stood in the center of a circle of silver. A larger silver circle hung in the air and she raised her son up toward it, bathing him in light.

"Artemis, goddess of women, teach him how to love. Let that be his journey."

Then she lowered him to her breast and died.

And then Jean-Marc walked in the same bower, a young man, weeping over the dying babe in his own arms.

"Forgive me, mon enfant," he whispered. "Lucienne, forgive me."

Jean-Marc knew how to love.

He had simply forgotten.

King Jean-Marc woke the next morning. His heart was aching and there were tears on his cheeks.

He walked to the reflecting pool just as dawn colored the water and humbly knelt before the statue of Artemis.

"I am done," he said. "I cannot force the Rose Bride to love me. And so, I will become a man she could love. A lovable man. A father to my subjects."

A lark trilled. The sun warmed Jean-Marc's face

and glowed on the face of Artemis. And did he see Rose's features there? Did the statue smile?

In his privy council, he called his advisors to battle. He told them they must wage a war against poverty and injustice as surely as the Pretender had hoped to wage a war against the Crown. They must educate the peasants and make sure they were safe and pro- tected. If need be, they must strike down nobles and warriors who abused power and privilege.

A week passed, and a year. King Jean-Marc found the widow and boy who had stolen a loaf of bread on the road. His name was Jean-Marc and the king made the boy his royal ward and gave his mother a house, a title, and piles of gold coins. Jean-Marc taught the young man how to ride and joust; Reginer taught him how to paint.

Rose watched Jean-Marc change. He flowered. His broken heart and his broken dreams slowly mended and healed. And she loved him all the more. He was a good man and a just king, and his journey had taken him far.

She knew he was beginning to forgive himself for that which he could not have prevented—the deaths of his wife and son. He was beginning to see the light.

She was no longer certain if her own heart was his destination. Time and life had changed them both. Perhaps her part in his life was to bring him to the light. Perhaps his eyes would gleam with true love for someone else. That was not for her to say. Love did not wait to see if it was returned. It simply existed, generously and fearlessly given.

So she held her counsel and bided her time. She played with her nephew and posed for Reginer. He painted a portrait of Artemis flying through the rose garden of the *château* . . . and if one looked carefully beyond the lovely young goddess and the fountain, one could see Rose, hunting with her goddess. They did not hunt deer. They hunted wishes. She hung the painting in her rooms. Few who saw it, saw her.

But Jean-Marc did.

And then on the night of her eighteenth birthday, there was a knock on Rose's door. Her maid ushered in a stooped old man and she knew him at once. He was Monsieur Valmont, who had been shipped off to the colonies to serve a lifetime sentence for the theft of her mother's dishes.

"*Monsieur!*" she cried, embracing him. She sounded like a young girl again and he, not quite so old. She led him to the fireplace and called for food and hot tea. "How did this happen?"

"The king pardoned me," he told her. His hand shook when he held the teacup. He was very feeble. "He sought me out and brought me here."

Rose's heart flooded with gratitude. She said, "You must live here as my guest and as my friend."

"The king has said as much," Monsieur Valmont assured her. He sipped his tea. "He reminds me so of your mother, kind and generous."

They spent the day and half the night reminiscing. She told him of the fate that had befallen Ombrine and Desirée, and she was surprised to find that he held no bitterness.

"The gods put us on our paths," he said. "If all that hadn't happened, we wouldn't be here now."

She was moved by his wisdom. She knew he was right.

It was near dawn when Valmont went to bed. Rose was blowing out the candles in her sitting room when was another rap on her door. She opened it to her brother, Reginer, who was in a state.

"Rose, Rose," was all he could say.

"Is it the baby?" she cried. He was practically mute. She touched his shoulder. *"Calme-toi, mon frère."*

He caught his breath as he shook his head. *"Non, non, ma belle,* it is the king! What an uproar. It seems His Majesty has gone mad."

She covered her mouth with her hand. "What are you saying?"

"He has been planting roses. Purple ones. All around the statue of Artemis. All night. Then he began shouting that the roses were speaking to him." He touched his forehead. "You see? *Fou!"*

"They . . . the roses?" she echoed, startled. Her heartbeat picked up as she looked at Reginer. "The purple roses?"

"Oui. He summoned Sabot and the privy council and told them to listen. Of course no one heard anything. He kept pointing at roses and saying, 'Don't

you hear it?' Of course they didn't. And now they've gone off to confer, to decide what should be done with him."

"I know what should be done," Rose said happily. She threw her arms around him. "Tell them to stay away. I will go to him alone."

"*Non*, he's crazy," Reginer insisted.

"How many miracles does it take to open your eyes to the work of the gods? Tell them to stay and give me leave to meet with His Majesty by myself."

And so it was done, the councillors pacing and anxious in the privy chamber, the courtiers beginning to gossip.

Rose put on a white dress and a gold cloak, and left the castle to walk to the reflecting pool. She had not gone there since the day of the great hunt when Jean-Marc had nearly killed her. She took no lantern to the birth of a new day. The moon guided her steps. And what she saw when she got there took her breath away.

The perimeter of the pool was lined with purple roses. The statue of Artemis stood above hundreds of blossoms, as if the goddess rode on purple clouds, shielded by purple canopies. Hundreds—thousands— of purple rose petals cascaded down from the lush bower . . . onto the dark, curly hair of Jean-Marc, king of the Land Beyond.

"*You are loved, you are loved, you are loved*," they murmured, kissing his cheeks, his lips, his forehead.

In his black-and-golden clothes, his head tipped back, he was whirling in a circle, his arms outstretched.

And the boy who became a prince who became a king rotated in a slow circle, laughing.

"*You are loved.*"

He looked over at her. His cheeks were wet with tears of joy.

He said, "I know it now." He reached out his hand. "I know it, Rose."

The moon glowed as the sun rose and she put her hand in his. "Then know me."

So of a night, the pair walked, as in the old days when she was enchanted. Every night, beneath the moon, they strolled around the pool and talked. People remarked on the closeness they shared. The warmth and humor. They laughed often. Jean-Marc taught Rose how to play the lute and to use a sword. She taught him how to grow vegetables and to forage for berries. They took care of little Laurent, giving his parents sufficient opportunity to make a sister for him. Her name was Clarisse.

Some said they could never be lovers because they were friends.

Then came the night of Rose's nineteenth birthday. She thought of her dearest mother, dead so long. She remembered Tante Elise and even her father. There was no bitterness that they were gone, only joy that she had known them. She felt such happiness that she thought she should be glowing like an emissary of the goddess. She was at peace.

Arriving for their walk, the king said, "Tomorrow

we'll feast your day. I think Laurent should have a new puppy, and Clarisse will get a kitten."

"Those are the best gifts I will receive," she declared.

"One hopes not," he said. He reached behind his back and offered her a single purple rose.

It was a moment and she knew it. She caught her breath.

He knelt. "Rose, my friend, *ma belle copine*. I know you now. You're my dearest friend in all this world."

"And you are mine," she replied. Her heart forgot to beat.

"You know very well that I will always love Lucienne. You know that I will always miss her."

"I do," she said softly. She touched his hair. It was as soft as a petal.

"And that I grieve so for Espere, my little son."

"*Oui*," she whispered. "I, too."

"Loving them in my imperfect, wounded way was the seed that has blossomed into the love I bear for you. For my people. For the world." He extended his hand. "My lady and my love, it is time. You know that it is. Please come into my garden as my true Rose Bride."

On the next full moon, they were married in the garden. Claire lovingly sewed the magnificent pink gown into inserts in the bridal dress. She attended Rose, baby Clarisse laughing in her mother's arms. Reginer, Velmont, and Jacques were the king's men, and little Laurent carried his aunt's ring. Three priestesses of Artemis and three priests of Zeus officiated. Rose wore

a white gown; Jean-Marc wore black and gold.
Coronets of purple roses encircled their heads.
Festoons of purple roses bound their wrists together.

True love's kiss took Rose back in time, to a night
of stars and roses when her mother made a wish.

True love's kiss took Jean-Marc back in time, to a
childbed and a mother who swore to love her son forever. To a son and a wife who proved that true love
could never die. It lived on in the heart of the beloved.

And as true love's kiss sealed king and queen
together, the statue of Artemis took on many guises,
her facial features shifting and altering—Celestine,
Elise, Marie, Lucienne.

"I have granted the wishes of my Best Beloved women,"
she said aloud, for all to hear. "The journeys I set their children on were in fulfillment of their prayers and not due to any
whim of mine. These two, who truly know what love is, are
the purple roses of the world. Their hearts are mended. May
they flourish forever. May they sow seeds."

She let her stone arrow fly into the air, and stars
cascaded down. The roses twinkled with fairy lights
and fairy tears of joy.

A tiny fawn stumbled in from the greenwood,
bleating, and wobbled up quite fearfully to the royal
couple. Rose knew it was the baby of the king buck,
who had mated with another. At the same instant,
Rose and Jean-Marc knelt down and gentled the shy
little creature. Rose took off her coronet of purple roses
and draped it around the graceful neck of the fawn.
Their magical scent soaked the air.

"You love," the roses whispered. *"You love."*

After Rose and Jean-Marc married, anyone with a gleam of light in their heart could hear the reassurance of the purple roses. *"You are loved, you are loved,"* they whispered to lord and lady, merchant and beggar. It lifted their souls to hear the words, and the light in their hearts grew brighter. So they planted purple roses of their own and more people listened. Those people in turn planted roses. The Kingdom of the Land Beyond became a shining, magical country, and people came from all over to bask in its joy and prosperity.

A daughter was born to the king and the queen, and they named her Marie-Cieline. The gown she wore when she was presented to Artemis was fashioned from the last bits of Rose's pink birthday dress, and Rose could almost see Marie-Cieline's grandfather, Laurent, coming home at last to hold the precious child.

All were home now, and the world shifted on its axis most perfectly, more beautifully, the star in the diadem of the Goddess of the Hunt and of the Moon as she beamed down on the Rose Bride, her emissary of love.

> *My bounty is as boundless as the sea,*
> *my love as deep.*
> *The more I give to thee, the more I have,*
> *for both are infinite.*
> —William Shakespeare

Author's Note

It is difficult to write about grief and loss when one is the mother of a fairy child. But by writing about the Rose Bride's journey, my hope was to show that while love may not conquer all, it can heal all. I think people who write (and read) feel deeply. Joy and despair are both very strong forces in us, and so I want to say to you, if your path seems too dark for you, fear not. Keep going. If you stop, you stop in shadow. If you move forward, you will find sunlight beyond the black. I know this for a fact.

Besides the miracle of my beautiful daughter, and the strong and enduring love of so many friends and family, I had a number of other sources of inspiration for this book. One was the film *Ever After*, directed by Andy Tennant and starring Drew Barrymore. Another was Jean Cocteau's 1947 version of *Beauty and the Beast*. While I wrote, I played *Changes Like the Moon*, a CD of evocative harp music by Judith Pintar. Last but not least, I am deeply grateful to my two writing mentors, Dr. John Waterhouse and Charles L. Grant. Rest in peace, Charlie, and thank you for everything.

ACKNOWLEDGMENTS

With gratitude to my acquiring editor, Emily Follas, and my inspiring editor, Sangeeta Mehta. Thank you so much, Sangeeta, for lavishing your time and attention on the garden of my story. You truly brought the roses to life.

And with deepest thanks to: Howard Morhaim, and his assistant, Katie Menick; my webmaster, Sam Devol; my local computer guru, Eugene Son, and Ashley McConnell, my dear friend. Abbie Bernstein, Karen Hackett, Linda Wilcox, Amy Schricker, and Beth Hogan. Susi Frant, Kym Rademacher, Terri Yates, Christi Holt, Margie Morel, Barbara Nierman, Ellen Greenfield, Pam Escobedo, Monica Elrod, and Liz Cratty. Craig Miller, and the fabulous Children's Programming at LACon IV: Amelia Sefton, Dana Ginsberg, Tanya Olsen, and Alison Stern. Charlotte Fullerton, Lisa Morton, and Ricky Grove. My dear Yayas: Leslie Jones Ackel, Anny Caya, Lucy Walker, and Belle, always and forever my Belle. Elise Jones, Sandra Morehouse, and Richard and Skylah Wilkinson. *Domo arigato gozaimasu*, Kuniko and Mahlon Craft. A butterfly kiss to sweet LJW. Thank you for tending

Bonnie Charlie: Doug Winter and Tom and Elizabeth MacDonald. To Steve Jones, for sitting down and really listening. Thank you, Andy Thompson, and everyone at Family Karate: Courtesy, integrity, perseverance, self-control, indomitable spirit. And to Brian Vernia, Belle's wonderful fourth grade teacher—I am forever in your debt.

About the Author

NANCY HOLDER

has more than seventy-eight books and two hundred short stories to her credit. Her books for Simon Pulse include the Wicked series and another book in the Once Upon a Time series, *Spirited*. Nancy also recently published the novel *Pretty Little Devils*. She lives in San Diego with her daughter, Belle, and far too many animals. Visit www.nancyholder.com.